Lessons in Paradise

By William Harrison

LESSONS IN PARADISE
IN A WILD SANCTUARY
THE THEOLOGIAN

Lessons in
Paradise

by William Harrison

William Morrow and Company, Inc. 1971

New York

This Book Is for My Mother
Who Wasn't Quite Like This
And, Once More,
For Merlee
Who Isn't Quite Like This Either

Life can only be understood backwards,
but it must be lived forwards.

—Sören Kierkegaard

≫ I ≪

It was a bright spring morning, the flowers of the Garden District were lush and open, and Baskin, unhappy with life among his numbers and equations, got out of bed slowly, dressed, and walked toward his laboratory at the university. Small premonitions rode around inside him, he felt fatigued, and his memory—that cavernous storehouse by which he lived—was spinning out of control. As he walked he peered up into the leaves arching overhead, into a deep foliage that was unmistakably New Orleans, yet he saw something else: a distant ranch, his mother, the vivid snow-tipped buttes, a high pasture, and the gray sweet clouds which always lingered down the length of the valley beyond his childhood house in Montana. His vision became so real and his preoccupation so intense that he stumbled off a curb, almost fell, and found himself standing dumbly in the middle of the trolley tracks.

All that morning, then, he sat in his cubicle at the lab playing with his dull equations and thinking about his mother.

Quickthought: sitting with her in the big lunchroom at the University of Chicago in 1957. I was eight years old and proud of forking in my food European style. Very cool eating habits. Mother sat across from me reading problems out of the trig book, watching the rhythm of my eating and waiting for my answers. She read me all those problems aloud so that I could work them in my head for her. Pleased, she offered to buy me another banana pudding and I accepted. Why all these problems when I'm eating? You know perfectly well you'll get indigestion if you don't occupy your mind while you eat, she answered. You'll get nervous tummy. No I won't, not really. Yes, you will. Drink your milk and concentrate on this one. Try to get the picture in your mind's eye as I tell you the equation. All right now, are you ready? Yes, ready.

The prodigy years. They've ended now, haven't they? I'm twenty years old. I'm Baskin, the rememberer, the warm computer, the genius. And registration of information and recollection have always been automatic with me, yes, but why do some thoughts bubble up all by themselves? Involuntary memory, yes, I know, but it always seems so unreal.

The cubicle where he sat had no window—something he resented—and so he got up several times from his work that morning and strolled around the labs. He had no assigned duties, no particular hours at the school, and taught no classes. As a researcher, he came and went in first one department and then another, helping them solve their problems, entertaining the professors with his calculating speed and memory tricks, working at his own problems when the fancy struck him. So no one paid much attention to his restlessness that morning.

Toward noon he felt a slight trembling in his hands, something he couldn't account for.

Quickthought: the wavelength at which maximum intensity occurs is given by the simple formula $\lambda max = 0.29$ cm/T.

He went to lunch at the Faculty Club. Two glasses of red wine (a little dribbled on the tablecloth), two pieces of chicken, a cup of cold fruit. He borrowed a cigarette from Professor Behrman, who asked if anything was wrong.

"N-no, I'm just a little jumpy. Spring fever, maybe."

"What are you working on this semester?"

"Physical chemistry. Oh, some equations of my own, as always. Writing a little p-paper, too."

"Too much work. Take a few days off, Baskin, and go down to the French Quarter. Indulge the flesh."

He suddenly remembered going bare-assed in Montana as a boy. There sat the ranch in all its splendid isolation and there was Sarah and her son with the all-over tans. All through those summers of cool air and warm sunlight we would lie on pillows on the glassed-in porch at the back of the house, books and journals strewn around, the light slanting across our bodies, or we would go across the meadows, always jabbering, of course, her large brown breasts gleaming in the warmth, small beads of perspiration gathering at her temples. The bottoms of our feet were leathery. I didn't cut my hair until I was five years old and then only occasionally, so I was a lion cub, quick of eye, in the high grass.

Lunch ended, Behrman giving him several good-natured forms of erotic advice which he acknowledged with a fixed smile. Then Baskin walked out across the terrace, down the walkways choked with students late for the first afternoon classes, and back to the lab.

Settling down to work, he broke a pencil lead. It promised to be a long afternoon. Dark thoughts hovered around the cubicle.

He began wondering as he had often wondered in the last weeks if his life had accelerated so that he approached a form of premature middle-age despair. That was all his genius was, get right down to it: mostly just speed. As a three-year-old, he could read the newspaper and had come to terms with triangles, Sarah's early math forms, and his first music appreciations; at four, he began finding quick methods of multiplication and wrote short stories about the animals up on the mountain; at five, he composed music, but by then, clearly, numbers were his game because everything else seemed infinitely slow and plodding; at seven, he made another trip down to the state university in Missoula with Sarah and she sat him before an examining board, the old gaggle of professors who weren't ready for him and who told his mother to bring him back, please, in two weeks, when they'd have suitable exams. They went to Chicago instead, and Sarah turned him over for the first time to others. But all this, he speculated, is just a story of acceleration, of many minor achievements in a short span of time. And where has it led? I'm not happy in this rote work and want to do something else, something only I can do, if possible, and not merely something I can do more *quickly* than some other person or machine. And is this what I feel these last weeks? Or is it the first twitch of mortality? Perhaps so: the end of hope and the beginning of resignation most men feel—usually later in life rather than this soon.

There's the question, all right: what is it I can do now with this paltry index brain and with this stupid speed?

He got up again and left the cubicle and went walking outside, pacing slowly across campus, across the trolley tracks again to Audubon Park where all the flowers of the city broke open their perfumes. He liked New Orleans in the springtime before the humid weather set in, but his thoughts were far off and he kept seeing the jagged peaks above the Montana ranch, the white ballast of snow on the barns and outbuildings, Sarah at her typewriter, sitting there in that pudgy slump of hers as she struck out the words that made their living. Her pudgy brown body: naked all summer and heavy with great, oversized mackinaws all winter. He pictured her in the kitchen at the stove, boiling pots all around her, odors of meat sauce and pudding ambushing him as he sat waiting at the table, his book splayed open. The agony of those odors! He got annoyed with her constant questionings, told her so, suffered them all the more, and waited for the food. And they were fat together: two Buddhas, paunchy and wise.

Alongside the lagoon running through the park the girls from the nearby universities and colleges sunned themselves on blankets and towels and Baskin thought of Sarah's nudism, smiling, thinking of her dumpy body, the dark patch of hair, the sag of her belly. She explained nudism, he remembered, as purely one of her eccentricities, not something he should especially take up for himself, but he always joined in when the weather wasn't nippy. His torso was round like hers, only more pale. Everyone who came to the ranch to visit joined in, too, and he remembered his earliest of early memories: searching through the clothes that hung in the bathrooms and wardrobes and closets while everyone padded around outdoors. Once he piled everyone's money in one pile. There must have been twenty guests or more, all of them outdoors ping-ponging and barbecuing, paying him no attention—he must have been four years old at the time—and when they came back inside there were many groans and admonishments and complaints, but Sarah was up to his tricks and said, Okay, Baskin, put it all back. And of course he remembered just how much everyone had, down to the last penny: the brown seersucker pants had seventy-eight cents in the right-hand front pocket (two quarters, two dimes, a nickel, three pennies) and the blue jeans had forty cents in change and ninety dollars in the alligator billfold.

Quickthought: Sarah's nudism: she wasn't at all cultish about it and never made speeches and for that matter there wasn't any literature or any picture magazines in the house. But a nudist she was, true, and so were her guests more often than not, most of the editors who flew out from New York, all the cowboys, all the old girl friends. It was a place of varisized and odd-shaped dear cunts and ding-dongs: the men flapping and dangling as they jumped around slapping the volleyball and the women all variously bushy and demure and the children, when occasionally there were other children, all bald and somehow sadly plain. More than nudism, as Sarah herself would explain to him, it was pantheism: the worship of the outdoors, all things natural and lovely. But don't get hung up on the theological implications of pantheism either, she warned him, because I'm a nudist, you see, Baskin, and a pantheist, indeed, but one mustn't work these things around too long in the mind. He took her at her word, then, and went bare-assed and enjoyed the mountains. There were far more engaging preoccupations.

Girls alongside the lagoon now. He looked at his watch. Three o'clock in the afternoon. Fourth of April. Premonitions.

At the edge of the water he saw his reflection there between the lily pads: shaggy head of hair, a Baskin less paunchy than as a child, decent looking, in fact, yet wearing a soft frown of melancholy.

He tried to think of something else to shake off the feeling that clung to him, visualizing the Crescent City in his map of thought. Names of lovely streets: Calliope, Carondolet, Royal, Esplanade. The curve of the river, the

14

mirrors at Galatoire's restaurant, the Streetcar Desire preserved near the French Market and the Café du Monde. As in all the cities where he had lived or visited, he knew the names of all the streets, the principal buildings and most of the shops in between, the number of city blocks and feet and inches in any direction from any given point. One of his games: to count things and to know, in a sense, exactly where he was at any given moment. At the moment, he could estimate that he was nine hundred and forty yards from the tip of the Gothic tower over at Tulane; nineteen hundred air miles from the Montana ranch; seven and one-half feet from his reflected image in the water of the lagoon. Yet, also, he asked himself, where exactly am I? Where in relation to my prodigy-ridden childhood? How many light-years from the self I could be? And what to do with myself now, exactly and precisely what?

He walked and mused. For more than a year, he said to himself in review, I've worked here as an interdepartmental researcher, a job they invented for me, yet it's a work I can do, that's the sad part, and in truth I'm just a damned oddity, a quirk of nature and Sarah's creation. And, besides, the charm of being a kid is finished. No longer when I multiply five figures by four figures in fifteen seconds do the professors grin and bear it. No more hands in my blond curls, no more candy bars. I'm getting cranky and going the way of all genius into mildly annoying eccentricity.

On campus again, he returned the nods of the students. That's proof there, he told himself: I'm known. I'm a public object. Since those first news articles put out by the PR staff at the University of Chicago years ago, I've been fair game. The students give each other sly looks when I stutter slightly, as if to say, Ah ha, watch him crack, all geniuses crack up, that's a well-known fact. And didn't Behrman imagine that he had a slight sexual advantage over me at lunch today, saying to himself, Well, what have we here? The virgin genius! He was good-natured about it, I suppose, but his voice had an edge of condescension.

Back to the laboratory. An odor of sulphur tinged the air. As Baskin took his place in the cubicle, he saw that his hands were shaking again.

If $T = 3°K$, then $\lambda max = 0.1$ cm and the radiation at this temperature is therefore in the form of radio waves and no other known astronomical source will contribute significantly to the radiation in these wavelengths.

Quickthought: once, near the end of my time at Chicago, when I was sixteen years old, out of sorts with Sarah because I felt she was being bitchy and didn't want to let me go, I went to see Professor Lothridge over at the Fermi Institute. He turned on the hot plate which sat atop his fancy walnut desk, heated water, and made us coffee. We talked for a long time—I stuttered a good bit, I recall—and then he said to me, "Baskin, there's only one ability worthwhile for you to develop now: the ability to perceive new relationships, new islands of order, some new *Gestalt*. And I don't think this is just something granted to an exceptional few. It's a way of seeing that's developed like almost everything else. If, as you say, you're getting tired of occupying yourself with speed tests and problems that require, oh, quick mental reflexes, you have to begin to train yourself to see things no one else can see. You ought to begin sharpening yourself for this sort of creativity." I remember being slightly defensive, Baskin told himself, because after all I had a few published papers to my credit, I had my accomplishments, some pride, too, but now old Lothridge's words come back. In the data of my life, I need to see some new configuration. Maybe this is what I'm feeling today, this longing for some new insight; perhaps this is what I've felt about myself these last weeks.

He sat in the cubicle feeling perspiration form on his wrists and forehead.

I'm not a moody person, he explained to himself. I'm not one of those middle-range geniuses who suffer emotional hang-ups, not at all. What was it Sarah explained to me? Ah yes: individuals with IQ's above 160 like you, Baskin, just don't succumb to the nervous breakdowns of lesser minds. All right, I accept that—but what is this I'm feeling? An emotional nausea, I'd say.

He got up and left the cubicle again.

Slightly disgusted with himself for being so restless, he still began to trust his premonition. Too many times his thoughts had leapt at something he couldn't explain; he had taught himself to try his hunches. Now, as he walked out of the building again, he let loose the worry boiling inside him, let his emotions free-fall so that perhaps he could somehow fathom them. Oh shit, he said to himself, this is awful. And for no reason at all he felt that a sob might escape his throat. His eyes burned and he stopped and leaned against the cold brick wall of the building.

Now the feeling came in waves—so strong that he struggled to recognize what was wrong with him—and through the blur of his vision he saw Dean Parmelee coming toward him from across the quad. Parmelee's bouncy walk, the forward cast of his head; Baskin knew him exactly and knew, also, that here it came. His vague emotional binge began to turn to certainty on him.

The loveliness of formulas: the beauty of that great cosmic black-body radiation at 3°Kelvin.

Dean Parmelee was at his side. He had coffee breath and clutched Baskin's shoulder.

"What is it?" the dean rasped at him. "Have you already heard?"

Baskin nodded yes. Of course he didn't know exactly, hadn't heard the words which the dean had intended to utter, had no idea of the telephone conversation which the dean had finished with someone at the ranch just moments before, yet his thoughts were pinwheeling along at blinding speed and he was receiving tremors in the afternoon silence of the campus and knew the feeling that bombarded him: it was grief. Never before had the gears of his mind shifted into such a strange, extrasensory latitude. But in that moment he knew that Sarah was dead.

That afternoon Baskin settled all his affairs in New Orleans. As always, he made up his mind quickly and tended to everything: his apartment lease, his job, even his overdue library books and his suit at the cleaners. Then he sat for a while in Dean Parmelee's office explaining how it was better this way, and Parmelee could only smile and agree, of course, and point out that the year was almost finished, after all, so that Baskin's duties didn't demand that he stay.

"You can change your mind, naturally," Parmelee told him. "You can always come back here—next fall—if everything gets straight for you."

But Baskin said no, that he was already feeling that such work wasn't right for him, that if it hadn't been Sarah's death something else would have given him the excuse for leaving the cubicle forever. "I just think my years as the boy computer are over with," he said, managing a smile.

Parmelee helped him with the last chores then: the arrangements for his last paycheck to be sent to Montana, a cashed check, the call to the movers. Baskin didn't go back to his apartment. He told Parmelee there was nothing there, only a few clothes and linens, and that he didn't want to see it again.

In the bar at the airport before Baskin's evening flight Parmelee tapped down a pipe of tobacco, ordered Manhattans, and urged Baskin into some conversation about his mother.

"She would have approved of me this afternoon," Baskin admitted. "She was a great one for shortcuts: all sorts of speed methods and direct routes."

"You may find that this was too sudden after all," Parmelee suggested for the last time.

Baskin said things were as they should be, smiled again to assure his dean, and watched Parmelee stir his drink. A jet roared to life out on the runway and they both turned absently to gaze at it through the tinted window of the bar. Baskin studied the old dean's profile, remembering that it was Parmelee who had created the position at the university, who had gained all the publicity and prestige for having signed him to a contract, and who alone had befriended him after he had agreed to come. There had been three afternoons out at Parmelee's house on the lake, dull sessions with the dean's dowdy wife, but Baskin had appreciated them; twice they had gone out for expensive dinners in the Quarter; one other time Parmelee had invited some of the young faculty to a supper party, mostly young lady instructors, and though the party had fallen flat, Baskin appreciated that too—appreciated it all. Under the circumstances, Baskin knew, Parmelee is a hero. I've been a cold fish, as always, unemotional, and the good dean has just tried to warm my life a little. He felt he should reach over and touch Parmelee's sleeve, do something finally personal, but sat fingering his drink instead.

They talked about Sarah. Parmelee remembered old newspaper accounts about Baskin's prodigy days when Sarah was the coach and entrepreneur.

"That's right, she took me all over the country. We performed for the combined science faculties of a dozen universities, I suppose."

"You were a famous little boy."

"When I was seven years old I used to read the feature articles in the newspapers about myself and judge them. Some were pretty banal."

"Your mother must have been some woman."

"There's something I won't get to ask her now," Baskin said.

"What's that?"

"I would like to have asked her how much she knew— in order to have taught me. It's a question I owed her, but I never asked."

They went down the concourse together, Parmelee carrying Baskin's briefcase. There wasn't much more to say, so they shook hands for several seconds and Baskin said, "G-good-bye," stuttering slightly, and got on board.

Strapped in his seat, his thoughts skipped back across the events of the day, the last months, then back across the years, and he sat there surprised at himself slightly for having said what he did about Sarah to Parmelee. Yet, it was true: there had been at least four or five occasions since he left the University of Chicago at age sixteen when he could have reached Sarah again, when he could have communicated to her that everything was all right between them again, and it would have been as easy as having reached over and touched Parmelee's sleeve in the bar.

Summary: eight years at that ranch, eight years alone with Sarah when it was just her and me and our thought-games and our books and our long conversations, eight years of Sarah as mommy. Then Chicago: eight more years, the difficult ones, when I was no longer Sarah's alone but part of many people, my professors and colleagues and acquaintances and admirers, and when Sarah and I became antagonists and fussy combatants. Then four years away from each other: the time spent at my jobs in New York and New Orleans. And now: Sarah's death. This: the exile's return, the long voyage back.

Summary: of course, long before this all happened there was Sarah alone in New York back in the days when she was a free-lance reporter, doing stories for the *Herald* and for *Collier's,* the *Saturday Review,* the *Post,* and occasionally *The Times*. This was just after the war, Baskin recalled, and he thought of the photos of Sarah which had been piled unglued into all those old scrapbooks in the ranch library: photographs of a slightly plump, always smiling, tough, randy girl reporter, her red hair swept back tightly on her head, a cigarette sometimes drooping from her lips, a face something like a fat Myrna Loy with the features set pleasantly apart, small eyes, a good nose. She was not particularly pretty, no, and that's why she went until she was thirty-one years old, perhaps, before getting seriously mixed up with a man. Of course, there was her career, Baskin felt, and the war. But more than anything the fact was that she was plump and plain and took refuge in her deadlines and interviews, in her individualism as a newspaperwoman among men.

The plane roared off the runway, soared up, leveled off. Baskin sat transfixed, looking out, and estimated their cruising speed at about four hundred.

$$Momentum = \frac{hy}{C^2} \times c = \frac{hv}{c}$$

Momentum and mass, the velocity of light, waves and photons: the memory is quicker than all these, Baskin knew, and images came roaring back now, particles of the past like cosmic dust, wisps of thought.

When Sarah became pregnant by Dierker—early 1949, the year was—of course they couldn't marry. Dierker had three children, a big house up in Ossining, and was jockeying for the presidency of his publishing firm. They were in love, but no matter; it was arranged for Sarah to leave New York, to go back to her parents in Montana, and to live out the poignancy of the separation. There was also money involved: a few thousand from Dierker—Baskin never found out exactly how much—and a contract for two Western novels, the quick-sell pulp variety, for which Sarah received the unusually high sum of $2000 in advances because of Dierker's influence.

Sarah decided to buy the ranch instead of living with her parents, and although Sarah's mother helped with the birth and for a few days afterward, it was soon just Sarah and the child. She wrote her books and tried to survive the winter. Then, amazingly, her first western, *Draw Poker,* sold 300,000 paperback copies. The next, *Winter Kill,* was serialized in the *Post,* sold 550,000 copies at 25¢ each, and was bought by Warner Brothers, never, unfortunately, to be made into the Errol Flynn movie that Sarah dreamed about. Yet, her new life was started and she would never go back to New York. The first winter with all its blowdowns along the ridges above the ranch, its heavy gray skies, the snow, the physical labor of washing and cooking and tending to the new baby didn't discourage her. In the spring, buoyant and pleased with herself, if a little fatter, she paid off the mortgage on the ranch, bought a new Jeep, a tractor, took an advance of $10,000 on the hardback edition of her third novel (because of the sales she had advanced in three books from a pulp writer to a "distinguished female author of western lore," according to a New York *Herald* reviewer), and began some permanent improvements on the living quarters.

Quickthought: Sarah didn't believe in introspection. She never mulled over herself and that pregnancy and that first tough winter she probably, in her way, enjoyed.

Baskin checked his schedule. He would arrive at the airport in Missoula, after all the intermediate stops, at approximately midnight. He gazed out into the gathering twilight.

That first summer after Baskin's arrival, from all he now understood of the things Sarah had said over the years, his mother decided to do something about her loneliness. She invited Dierker and others from New York to come for a visit, and they came. It was mostly for sex, Baskin supposed, yet not altogether. They did take off their clothes, yes, but it was more matter-of-fact than an orgy, very much like those later summers Baskin could recall for himself when there was less exhibitionism than love of the outdoors and good humor. Sarah was awfully plump, for one thing, and didn't inspire an atmosphere of sexuality and the erotic; the men were also worn with the long New York winters, soft in the gut from too many business luncheons at the better French restaurants where the editors and agents gathered, pale of skin, and tender of foot. There was little else to do except laugh at themselves when they first stripped down during their summer visits, Baskin remembered, and they always did laugh—and probably did that first summer which hung outside even the vaguest of his infant memories. But Sarah ended her isolation that summer, whatever, and never again would she do without friends. In the winters she and Baskin would mostly stay at the ranch while she undertook his education, occasionally going back to New York to visit and make a deal on a new book and occasionally going down to Mexico or the Virgin Islands or even, once, over to Europe, and then in the summers there would be a lot of people, a constant party of a dozen guests, lots of food and late evening talk, horseback riding and hikes and sometimes even other children for Baskin. This was the schedule for all those eight years: a winter of books and Sarah's speed methods and clothes followed by a summer of houseguests, social occasions, food, and nakedness.

"You know we can't come to New York now," she used to say into the telephone. "We're busy with Baskin's studies. No, of course not. He never attends school. I don't want school interfering with his education!"

If that first summer of visitors was essentially a sexual adventure, even so, Baskin could understand it. The ranch was a lonely place, the house set out at a desolate distance from other houses, miles from town, and Sarah had only a child to talk to, so that her loneliness probably intensified. She needed men, a toss in bed, conversation, all those things. She used to stand at the window, a wide expanse of snow outside, drumming her fingers lightly as he rattled off his reading assignments, and he wondered, now, what all that solitude and loss of adult companionship did to her. Did it drive a wedge into her character? Was she more than those silly cowboy novels which she dashed off? Of course she was, but how much more? Alone in this plane, stranded high above the country, suspended for a moment between one destiny and another, the question beset him.

Sex, yes: there might have been a mild promiscuity in it all. But only mild. Dierker's friends, a lot of them—no doubt of this—came to the ranch out of curiosity, as one might go to any nudist colony. But when the clothes were heaped in the closets and wardrobes everything was suddenly more tribal than sexual—or at least seemed that way. Sure, they made love. There were many jokes about mosquitoes, jokes he always only partially understood as a child. Sometimes there were jealousies he detected. And, once, true, he had witnessed the act itself. That was out in the stable—he must have been about seven years old, mature enough, anyway, to be interested in such recreations—when he looked down from the rafters where he was playing and climbing, at a Jewish girl named Melissa and good old Dierker. They had come in from riding. Of course they wore jeans while in the saddle, and boots and shirts as well, so in the process of getting undressed —they were laughing and giggling a lot, he recalled— they got all tangled up in that narrow stall with Melissa's big roan. The best of it Baskin saw gazing down silently from his perch in the rafters, peeking around the horse tack hung below, was that Melissa got to admiring the roan's penis and took it in her hand and she and Dierker were laughing and she just leaned over the horse's backside and exposed her own while Dierker went to work on her. He's intercoursing her, Baskin remembered thinking. Intercoursing her rear end, I guess, right there across old Rooster (the name of the roan) and, ha, what's she doing with the horse? He scarcely breathed.

Of course it was sex, much of it. But more than all this, the ones who came to the ranch had an inerrant sense of themselves, of the place, of their coming together as a group. It was not an open *salon*. Of the perhaps two dozen visitors who came to the ranch all those summers, there were no bores. Perhaps, alone, somewhat like Sarah herself, they were bores; but on the ranch they comprised

26

a nameless and always interesting group, somehow beautiful. Friends: that's what they were. Something *I've* never had, Baskin allowed, and he listened to the drone of the jets. The window beside him had darkened and he caught sight of his reflection in it.

Food: ah, they were mostly fat friends, or became that way over the years. The meals were long communion periods. In the evenings when it was too cool to cook outdoors, they all dressed to the hilt and sat around the big walnut dining table on the porch. The fare was good, but not first-rate cuisine except when one of the New Yorkers brought a visiting chef or when Sarah did one of her specialties: Veal Rib Chops Milanaise, *Côtelettes d'Agneau de Lait Farcies à la Périgueux,* or, when available, the Montana specialty, Pilaff of Moose. Sometimes the men wore tuxedos. There was always fine wine brought in by the case from the East, and my limit, Baskin recalled, was one glass with dinner. Food was such a big thing out there, a way of surviving so much, even boredom, and the summer meals were deliberately festive. Everyone tried hard at mealtimes, tried to talk deeply, seriously, humorously, stylishly, and afterward, occasionally, the adults would dance, holding each other fondly but somewhat formally, the women's gowns crinkling, the men still keeping up the conversation as they glided around, their heads thrown back now and then in laughter. Then, later, when the wind picked up and the cold air came bristling down from the snowy peaks above them, the fire would be built up and the favorite desserts—usually hot cherry pudding or trays of *pannequets meringués*—and liqueurs would be brought out. Fat time, Dierker always called it. Baskin would usually fall asleep, pillowed and buried in quilts, in front of the hearth. He sometimes cleaned the dessert leftovers while everybody talked on. But then sleep: my strange, good moments, he mused, when I had the great pleasure of falling asleep while friendly adult voices surrounded me.

Baskin was served dinner by the stewardess, then let his head fall back for a short nap. When he awoke it was as if no time had passed.

Sarah: she was more than the gilded summer lady, he told himself, or the grand hostess. There was that other winter self, yes, and all those hours with our books. How deeply did the men, Dierker and the others, who she contended never hurt her, actually bruise her life? Were there scars from her early years that set her brooding on those long winter nights? Didn't she have artistic longings and didn't she hate those formula novels she cranked out—twenty-seven in all—over the years? So many questions loom up at the end of a life, but in Sarah's case especially.

No doubt of one thing, though, Baskin knew: I was her passion.

It was the winter of 1954 when she wrote to the Educational Testing Service and received the Stanford-Binet materials. She administered the tests herself, two of them, two weeks apart. For a while after that, Baskin remembered, she brooded over the results, and when I asked her what score I had she wouldn't tell me. At last she called Hoving, one of Dierker's friends who taught at Yale, and told him that she wanted to bring her son East to be tested again, but Hoving said no, that he'd arrange a session down in Missoula at the psychology department there.

It was down in Missoula that Baskin remembered first hearing himself talked about. He was just four and a half years old at the time and sat in the professor's office with Sarah, his legs dangling off the chair as he ate a small bag of peanuts he had asked Sarah to buy for him.

"What score did you get?" Sarah asked.

"We scored him—well, at an even two hundred," the professor answered.

"Now do you believe my earlier tests?"

"I'm very sorry to have said what I did earlier. You obviously did everything right when you administered the test."

"Well, what do I do now?"

"I don't know," the professor admitted. He shook a cigarette out of his pack and lit it. "Tell me a couple of things about him. When did he begin to read, for instance?"

"About a year ago. For a while I showed him words in his picture books, but then one day he just began reading. I know you won't believe this, but I really didn't help him. He just started."

"What does he read now?"

"Ask him."

"What do you like to read, Baskin?"

"Oh, I like maps."

"What else?"

"Any big book."

"What do you mean? Big, thick books?"

"Yessir."

"Why?"

"Because they're m-more important."

Those long winter nights between his fourth and eighth birthdays had been filled with projects, mostly entertaining ones such as the medieval castle he built out of cardboard, copying exact details out of one of his pictorial histories, everything laid out to scale, including the armor of the little knights which he made out of tin cans. Yet now he wondered about Sarah on such evenings. Where was her inner life? Did she burn? Behind her dreams for him, for the genius son, were there other dreams all dark and lost? She used to write many letters to her friends, he knew, and they never answered as often or as well as she hoped. She was a mail hawk, going down to the mailbox on the road before the delivery truck came around every day, usually sorting the bills after the delivery, looking in vain for the letter she might have been expecting. Or on those winter evenings when she made him climb up to bed in his loft—the closed, dear loft where he slept alone with his storybooks and games and baseball cards—he' would sometimes hear her creeping around the house below, restless footsteps, a shuffling, sad movement.

All this came to mind because he knew how different he was from Sarah. She was emotional, he was mostly not; she had deep, hot currents in her life, always, while he ran on a cool white heat, a tough detachment.

There was much else to think about: the baseball games in Chicago, the men she knew there, all those anguished years as the two of them grew apart, the futile returns to Montana as they tried to recapture something together, the arguments. The time she threw his notebooks downstairs after him. The condescension of his professors toward her—which he both welcomed and detested.

He was feeling all this when the plane started its descent into Denver. The captain crooned them a memorized pitch about their trip, the temperature in Denver, and the airline's best wishes.

Baskin sat there, his safety belt still fastened, and realized that he didn't even know how Sarah had died.

When he got off to change planes for the last leg of his trip, he could smell the mountain air and feel the ridges towering nearby, and some old sensations began to creep into him.

In the terminal he put in a collect call to the ranch. "Who is this?" he asked when someone said hello.

It was Kate McCluskey, one of his mother's friends.

"I'm calling from Denver," he told her. "En route. Was it you who called my dean this afternoon?"

She said yes and asked when he'd get to Missoula.

"Near midnight. Look, I'll get the flying service to bring me on up to Kalispell. Can you or someone else meet me there?"

The talk got involved. Kate said that she'd call Missoula and try to make reservations for him, and they talked about his renting a car if the flying service wouldn't run him up that late at night. Kate said she didn't like light planes up in the Flathead country after dark.

"Who else has arrived?" Baskin asked.

Several of the old gang, she told him, and, yes, Dierker was there, and, yes, there were plenty of people to help. There was a problem with the funeral, though, she explained, because Sarah left instructions that she wanted to be buried in a natural state: no embalming, no cosmetics, no casket, just dropped into the ground, and already some men had come up from one of the funeral homes in town—the hospital had notified them—and Baskin was needed to settle matters.

The loudspeaker in the terminal was calling his flight number, and outside the booth where he was talking a boy in a turtleneck shirt was impatiently waiting.

"Kate," he finally managed to ask, "how did she die?"

There was a patch of silence. "Cancer," Kate answered him with a tinge of uncertainty. "The cancer. So you really didn't know?"

He recovered slowly. "No, I didn't."

Promising that he would be there to take care of things

31

in a few hours, he said his good-byes, hung up, and went out to his next flight.

He sat down in the plane stunned. So, there it was: cancer. How long, he wondered, has this been going on? Weeks, months, since I saw her last? And suddenly a vignette tumbled into his thoughts, a scene he and Sarah had endured back in Chicago just before he took his doctorate that last semester. He was sixteen years old. Sarah had gone to the commencement exercises, had stood with the audience for the ovation when Baskin was presented with his hood, and then she and Baskin went out to eat and as so often that year fell into an argument. She raged and Baskin frowned and tried to deliver up a few crisp, mildly sardonic parries—as he always did. He couldn't recall what the argument was about, but he remembered how icily he ended it, telling her that he had a job in New York and was going there without her.

"I'll follow you there if I damn well please!" she shouted at him.

"If you do, that's all right," he answered. "You have your friends there and I can't stop you, but I'm living alone. It's no use between us."

"Listen, you little shit, you've got problems you haven't even dreamed of yet!" She continued yelling.

People all around the restaurant turned toward them.

"If I've got problems," he said, tapping his temple with his forefinger, "the answers are all in here."

She rose up suddenly, knocking over her wineglass. "You can handle things mathematically, Baskin, but let me tell you something. You shouldn't fool yourself. You shouldn't let yourself believe that you understand anything because of that. You *don't!* You understand *nothing!*"

⇾ III ⇽

In the shaky little Cessna that took Baskin on the last leg of his trip from Missoula to Kalispell that night, he realized that his emotions were jarring loose. A simple thing forced the realization: he was awfully scared. The snowy ridges and buttes were just below, as if he and the tobacco-chewing pilot could reach out and pluck a snowball off one of the high meadows.

Yet, he had flown in these shaky planes over these mountains before, so why, he asked himself, were his hands trembling now? Up inside himself he felt a thaw, as if his deepest emotional waters were trickling down on him. Since those last days in Chicago when he fought so much with Sarah, he had kept himself cool and reserved; now, perhaps, her death, the trauma of leaving New Orleans so quickly and this lonely, wobbly flight all did their work on him.

"S'gonna be all right, son," the pilot said out of the side of his mouth.

"I'm fine," Baskin lied, and he felt the slight condescension on the part of his pilot. The pilot knew exactly who he was, of course, and it was the same as ever: everyone enjoyed getting a slight physical advantage over an egg-head, over Sarah's genius son.

He felt the thaw, then, in himself. But he didn't expect what was coming when he landed in Kalispell.

As he climbed out of the plane and began to help with the baggage, glacial winds whipped his lightweight clothes. Green tinted snow bordered the runway lights and off in the distance he could make out the lights of Kalispell, but more than any particular sight or sound he could feel the cold familiarity of the mountains nearby. By the time they were trotting toward the hangar with the luggage Baskin's fingers were numb and the pilot was cursing under his breath.

There was a woman at the hangar, waiting for them just outside the door, dressed in a parka, her face shadowed under the hood. "Baskin?" she asked, and he nodded, his breath white in front of him, and she held the door. "Get in here quick. Aren't you freezing? Have a good flight?"

"Kate?"

"That's right. Don't you remember me? Come inside!"

They struggled through the narrow door of the hangar, suitcases bumping, Baskin shaking snowflakes off himself.

A round of awkward introductions followed as she offered them brandy and as the pilot lifted the flask Baskin looked over at Kate who was looking at him—and his thoughts went suddenly blank, white and empty as the field of snow out beyond the hangars. She had thrown back the hood of the parka, leaving her face framed in dark hair. The gaze she gave him: he stopped breathing, he imagined, and in the vast catalog of his head he had no place for the silly thought that came. She's looking at me. What to do? He felt flushed and foolish and began paying elaborate attention to the business at hand by way

34

of covering up. "Let's get this matter of the trip settled," he said almost brusquely to the poor pilot.

The pilot shuffled his feet and overcharged his passenger, but agreed to take the luggage out to Kate's Jeep. Baskin floated through the conversation, not paying much attention, counting out the money, trying not to look at Kate. She seemed younger than the woman who had been his mother's friend and confidante back in Chicago, but that was four years ago or more; he wondered if, at age sixteen, he had simply overlooked Kate, or had the gap in years simply narrowed, or what?

"Much snow on the Northfork Road?" he managed to ask her.

"Not much when I left the ranch," she said, "but we've had a flutter here in Kalispell for four hours now." He felt that if she didn't stop looking at him so directly he'd laugh like a schoolboy. Ridiculous.

He asked the pilot where they could drop him, and, yes, just put the bags in back, please, and sit down there: all this rendered in an even more abrupt way, so that Baskin suddenly remembered how Sarah taught him to overcome his awe of the hotels where they visited by ordering the bellboys and doormen around.

Kate stared at him, smiling, then slipped behind the wheel as Baskin gave her a terse warning. "Careful," he said, "this looks icy." He was almost military now.

It was after they had dropped the pilot at his hotel and started north in the Jeep that Baskin began to recollect anything about Kate. She was, of course, his mother's drop-in friend, the one who left their Chicago apartment riddled with stubbed-out cigarettes, lipsticked coffee cups, and minor observations and advice on those long, gray, dull afternoons when he would be at his desk in the corner room or standing at the blackboard which hung in the kitchen. Yet, now, his perfect memory tripped: was this the same one? what has she done to herself? where did these eyes come from?

As they drove, she told him about changes at the ranch: a new bunkhouse down at the river's bend, some alterations at the main lodge. Swirls of snow outside insulated them and he was intimidated by her slight perfume, her proximity, the closeness of her voice in the small cab of the Jeep. At his elbow a plastic panel flapped noisily and sent a pinpoint of cold air into his thigh.

Changes at the ranch, repairs and additions. He listened with a certain sad disbelief because Sarah had gone on living without him exactly as he had told her to do. Yet there was a sting of pain: the cancer he hadn't known about, the letters gone unwritten, this woman who had occupied his place.

"T-tell me," he began, less abrupt now. "How long have you been at the ranch? It slips my mind." (Slips the mind, never. I never knew.)

She began, thankfully, the whole story, how there had been all these men in her life since her earliest teens, how she had been content for so long in just being a woman among men, just a carrier of her sex, she put it, with a plumage of clothes and a practiced coyness, all the things men expected of her. She spoke with a solid familiarity, as if Baskin were her old, lost acquaintance, all the while peering up the road as the snowflakes came at them. He watched her fingers on the wheel.

Then more facts for him to file away: her first marriage, her college career after that early failure, the short spell after that during which she "copyread and decorated" for a suburban newspaper in Chicago, another marriage that ended in divorce because of her husband's many girl friends, then a retreat: a brief visit to Mexico, other jobs,

36

a sudden solitary existence. He didn't know where this gush came from, why she let go, but he was glad of it. "Then I met Sarah, you see, just as you were heading down the stretch studying for your prelims and spending all your time at the institute. She was spying on you. Making sure everything was going all right, though you kept telling her to leave you alone. Anyway, I was there, very disillusioned, and I answered Sarah's ad, and there I was, talking to her on the phone and here I am. I was in New York with her—I don't think you even knew *she* was in New York, but she still kept track of you for months after you took your first job. Then we came back out here."

They passed Columbia Falls by the time all this came out. Ahead, though Baskin couldn't yet see it in the snow and darkness, lay the Flathead range. No other town— just the Polebridge Store—was between Columbia Falls and the ranch in those next thirty miles. The street lamps of Columbia Falls came and went and Kate's voice was still there and he could breathe her perfume beside him. Horses, she was saying. She took care of the horses at the ranch.

"I knew nothing about them, but Sarah taught me," she said, and he answered, yes, Sarah was a great teacher.

"Do you know Dierker?" he asked her.

"Oh yes," she allowed. "Doesn't everyone who knows Sarah also know Dierker?"

"Does he still come to the ranch?"

"Sometimes."

"He's already at the ranch, did you say?"

"That's right."

"He's my father. Did you know that?"

"Of course I know that."

They began to drive in silence, Baskin trying to decide

how to regard her. The hills and curves of the Northfork Road began now and soon they would be following the route of the river, that wide, shallow Flathead, partially frozen, and suddenly Baskin's fantasies fell loose, and he saw lovely Kate, parka slipping away, stripped and naked, down on the banks of that river, a summer sheen flashing off her body, the sun baking them, and he saw himself with his hair long again running down the length of the meadow. Her eyes: alert and black and quick, seeing right through me. I can't believe this, he told himself, and he thought of other girls and of course there were none, never, only nights when he felt himself about to explode in all his shut-tight rooms, so many of those awful apartments filled with the furniture of loneliness in New York and New Orleans and even Chicago five or six years ago when he used to sit at his window doing equations in his head, addled with insomnia, sick at heart, his pajamas filled with a monstrous erection, his thoughts and dreams traveling at the speed of light. Measurements of the speed of light confirm that it is a constant c independent of the relative velocity of the light source and the receiver. Et cetera.

Kate was talking on, telling him about those who had congregated at the ranch.

The perfume allowed him to regard her with only mild detachment. She had taken his place with Sarah at the ranch, she had shared a secret, Sarah's illness, and had probably made up her mind concerning him. Did she know how he and Sarah used to fight? Did she know how awful their split had been? Where were her sympathies? At least she's talking on, he assured himself, and he took some satisfaction in how she had divulged so much about herself, all her marriages and trials. He watched her long fingers, her mouth, and breathed the perfume.

They had reached the narrow part of the road where they had a sheer drop of about forty feet into the river on their right side and a deep trench and a solid rock wall on their left. Snow wavered before the headlights and Kate slowed down, changed gears, then finally stopped altogether, saying, "Sorry, I just can't see exactly what's ahead."

Baskin got out, waded ankle-deep in the snow, and peered ahead. The canyon moaned with a fierce wind, blowing huge snowflakes into his eyes and he squinted to see.

"N-no wonder you couldn't see," he yelled back at her. "We're at a snowslide. Not twenty feet from it. The whole r-road is covered!"

"We'll just have to turn around, then," Kate said, putting the Jeep into reverse. Baskin was at her opened window, reaching inside to place his hand on hers.

"It's not that easy," he said. "There's nothing behind us except our tracks. I'm afraid we shouldn't have come this far tonight."

"Where are we? Can you tell?" Her voice was tinged with enough apprehension so that she definitely understood: small miscalculations were never tolerated by the stubborn Northfork winters.

"We're about six miles south of Hay Creek," he said, slipping in beside her again. Then, to soothe her: "Relax. We'll think about it for a minute."

Obediently, she shook a cigarette from her case and lit it. Then as they sat listening to the wind sweeping down the canyon he became struck with time and space, how quickly everything had turned on him, how he was suddenly gone from his tropical strolls around Audubon Park and his dull scribblings in his carrel, removed to this winter dream again—and a dream both old and new, it was

—and to this woman, also old and new; and life imitated his experiments, his playful, hypothetical activities in the carrels and labs: things went along, drifting, mildly serene, then suddenly the breakthrough came, the equation balanced, the change occurred and things would never be the same. Quickthought: horses. Old Rooster. Copulation.

"The problem is finding a place to turn around, but I think I have things in order," he finally announced, thinking out loud. "It won't be easy because of the drifts on the road, but we'll have to back up until we find a place to turn around." He smiled over at her, but she didn't smile back; in fact, she sighed impatiently. Danger annoyed her, he supposed, and he got out, positioned himself, and gave her hand signals while she edged slowly backward. Minutes later his feet ached with the cold, his thin summer trousers clung to his legs like cold tissue paper, yet he went on directing her, moving her in reverse, his thoughts in reverse, too, all muddled and rich with fantasy: Kate in summer, the two of them up at that lonely ranch, out in the stable perhaps, or in the loft, his old baseball cards strewn around, her brown legs apart.

Finally he stopped her. "Let me have the wheel now," he told her, "and I'll turn us around."

She climbed out, peeved, to look things over for herself. "You can't see a thing," she complained. Although her mood had shifted and she was showing her apprehension (cigarette snapped away into the snow with a tiny hiss), he wanted to grab her and hold her close until their cheeks warmed together.

"Let me have the wheel," he ordered her. The crisp manner again.

She said the obvious. "If you get off to the right, you'll go all the way down into the river. If you get off to the left, you'll hit the ditch, get stuck, and we'll still freeze."

"I know all that. Step aside."

"We can walk off some paces in that snowdrift and make sure, can't we?"

"I remember this place in the road," he said. "There's a wide space right over there."

"What if you don't remember? You haven't been up this road for years! Let's walk off the paces."

"I remember!" He didn't mean to shout exactly, but forced his voice against a gust of wind. "Stand aside."

She obeyed, sulking.

Anger: well, here's another emotion coming loose in us, he decided. Just what we need.

She was visibly irritated and called at him across the few steps that now separated them in the deafening wind. He couldn't hear what she said, so moved closer. "We could freeze to death for your pride in your memory," she said. Then with another tone, though necessarily loud in the howl of wind, but rich with condescension: "At *least* walk off the paces!"

He lost his patience with her and came right to her face, a move so sudden that even he didn't expect it of himself. "I don't forget! Anything! Remember that!"

She threw off her parka hood with rage. "As far as I'm concerned, you've forgotten everything that could ever be important!"

He bit his lip and turned away, going back to the Jeep. All this seemed like a pantomime of the past, an old film broken loose and flapping at the back of his memory.

"I know I watched your mother stand out on this road a thousand times waiting for just one letter from you," she called after him. "Three years I watched her! As far as I'm concerned, you're forgetful as hell."

His heart broke like an icicle. "Oh, stop it now," he managed, and his voice cracked, and he sat there momentarily, the Jeep's door ajar, Kate a few cold feet away, snow billowing between them, and for an instant he could feel his eyes grow hot. He clutched the steering wheel. Hours ago in New Orleans, leaning against the side of that building, premonitions waylaying him, it wasn't as bad as this. But then he straightened up, took charge of himself, and turned the Jeep around in a perfect U-turn.

"Get in," he commanded her, and she paused, pulled her parka back in place, then climbed inside.

He drove slowly back down the canyon. Silence between them. The snow moved in heavy drifts now and the tracks of the tires were already dim in outline. He wanted to let go, to pour out everything he wanted to say, to tell Kate to forget it, but he did nothing except sit there recalling Chicago, how his relationship to Sarah was always an emotional game—not unlike this little hassle with Kate now—and how they used to spar and parry and thrust at each other, he and Sarah, as if they were searching out weaknesses, and how they haggled over the big and the little, and how she bitched and raged and how he fought her off with his poise and cool until, at last, his emotional currents began to jam and he simply had no more feeling, no hostility, no repressions, no fear, no frustration with her, nothing.

"I've never seen it snow like this," Kate remarked dumbly.

Is the emotional life and every relationship like this, he asked himself, where you always have to play games, win advantages, and score psychological points?

Welcome Home, Baskin. Enter the City of Risk and the Misty Flats of Other People.

He thought of his old cubicle there in the chemistry lab back in New Orleans: how perfectly safe. Equations and daydreams: how simple and secure.

With the snow whirling around them, they made their way across a field to the Addison place, leaving the Jeep abandoned on the road.

The drifts piled high now and the blizzard that had generated high around the Arctic Circle swept down the Rocky range, across the silent blue glaciers, down the Flathead valley toward the rest of the state. In the slow eddies of the river where once Baskin and Sarah had cut their blocks of ice for storage, the indolent current was freezing solid. In the forests, tamaracks creaked under the sudden weight of ice and snow, great limbs occasionally breaking loose and coming down in clouds of snowdust while an elk, relentless and stolid, standing in some mountain crevice out of the wind, listened to the sound.

Baskin pumped his legs high in the snow, cutting a path across the meadow for Kate to follow.

"Are you sure that's the Addison place back in those pines?" she called, but he plodded on without answering.

⚞ IV ⚟

There was no one at home at the Addison lodge, but the door had been left unlocked, so they went in and built up the fire. Baskin's feet throbbed with cold; he found a pair of old man Addison's woolen socks, put them on, and planted himself in front of the hearth. Kate made a pot of coffee, edged it into the coals, and tried unsuccessfully to call the ranch.

Silence hung between them during all this.

Baskin sat shivering, feeble from that long trek across the meadow. His body, he realized, would betray him every minute in this country, would be soft and clumsy and inept, and he sat contemplating how it was still mostly round, altogether too white, accented with blond hair: the sum of months in libraries and those stupid cubicles. He wondered if anyone still went around in the buff up at the ranch.

"I'm sorry about what I said out on the road," Kate finally said, standing beside him and peering into the fire. "It was just our predicament: I was scared and didn't know if you knew what you were doing and it just all came out."

He made a casual gesture with his hand by way of ex-cusing her.

She bit her lip. For a long time, then, they didn't say anything else while the pine logs snapped and sizzled. Then, in spite of himself, he was thinking about sex again, and the fantasy about Kate in that summer meadow came once more, got dismissed, came again. He reconstructed that first moment when they met at the hangar, how she looked right into him, and why did she tell me all those personal things about herself so soon during our drive up here, he asked himself, and she must feel something for me because she lost her temper, isn't she thinking about me now and hasn't she given me thought lots of times? Ah shit, my body: a softwhite pillow. And hers: a long brown willow. Think on something else, anything. Some-thing Newtonian: every particle in the universe attracts every other particle with a force directly as the product of the masses of the two particles and inversely as the square of their distances apart. Et cetera.

Kate was talking and he caught the phrase "I *am* sorry" and wasn't really listening to her.

"How long did you know Sarah?" he finally asked, looking up at her.

"Five years, a little more."

Her profile: a bit too much nose, but there, facing the hearth, a dear sweet profile, soft breasts in a mound of cashmere, another precious mound there at the front of her ski pants. Get your mind clear.

"I knew her sixteen years," he said. "I ate, oh, let's see, just over fifteen thousand meals with her and I knew all her tricks and all her lovers and—now listen to this, Kate —I learned her lessons and her elations and her bitching. I learned everything she was."

Kate didn't answer.

45

"Well, here's my point," he went on. "You knew her only a short time—as a kind of patron, right?"

"She was a great friend. And taught me a lot, too."

"She was good to you—I know that."

"Very good to me, that's right." Kate sat down on the footstool and took off her wet shoes and socks. The straps of her ski pants dangled over the lovely curve of her feet. Baskin's fantasies gathered like high, floating, eerie clouds up the far reaches of his brain.

"B-but there: the two of you had one of those pleasant introductory relationships. She helped you leave New York, she helped you with your writing, and you took care of the h-horses, and it was all neat, just like that, right?"

"It was like that at first, yes, but we grew closer. I can't *convince* you of that—and why should I?—but we were close."

"And you went on a few trips?"

"Some. She went all the time—someplace or another."

"And in the summers Dierker and the old crowd came up for visits. Horseshoe games and all that, right?"

He was aware of snapping slightly, pushing his advantage, as he sat watching her feet in the swimming firelight.

"Please, Baskin," she finally said. Her tone softened somehow and he decided, ah well, say something conciliatory. But she got up, moved across the room, unzipping her sweater as she went, and disappeared into the front bedroom. His addled thoughts zoomed. A force field is determined by—by what? Suddenly all the rooms of his bachelorhood lurched before him, parading by in tatters of image: strewn socks, scattered phonograph albums, empty cans and bottles, all those furnished rooms and all those carrels and cubicles where he had studied, moaned, and sterilized himself with his intellectual fog. Speak, he was telling himself. Never mind that she's taking off her clothes. Say something brightly casual.

But Kate was talking again, her words tumbling beside his thoughts, and he picked her up in mid-observation as she was saying, "It started with that newspaper ad, sure, but your mother wasn't one for random relationships. She made friends—one way or another."

"She w-was like that."

"It certainly wasn't that I needed money from her, don't think that. I just needed someone to trust, someone who would tell me the truth, too, about how bad a writer I was." She explained all this to the flames, not looking at him, standing there in Mrs. Addison's faded chenille robe which had been knotted tightly and yet fell open and clutched around her all at once.

He tried to nod, yes, sure, I'm listening, but her waist was a mere wisp. How old is she? In her thirties?

Thankfully, she went on talking. She wanted to explain about Sarah and herself once and for all, he supposed, but he only half heard her, and if she swam in her feelings—being defensive with him—he certainly went splashing and freestyling in his own. The quickthoughts dizzied him: that campus seven long years ago, all those creamy coeds strolling in exotic swaying visions behind his eyes as he tried to concentrate on a page of scribbled equations, his genitals exploding, Sarah giving him that birthday party at the Faculty Club with his professors in attendance and the cake all pink and ignited and his heart going like a piston for that little student waitress with her missing blouse button who kept moving around their table. His twelfth and thirteenth years: oh, he had wailed to himself, will my prick ever get decently soft, and, oh, god, it gets stiff at the sight of trees, at the curve

47

of automobile fenders there along the Midway Plaisance, at the gentle movement of slide rules. If you knew how precocious I've been, Aunt Kate, and how vivid and rank my dreams have been.

She talked on, talking about Sarah's understanding of nature now, how much being out in Montana had done for her, and Baskin wanted to laugh, wanted to say, oh, you are nature, good Kate, and truly endowed: mountainous under that drab chenille, all valleys and landscapes, canyons and crevices to break the heart.

"I'll try to phone again," she said finally, and he watched her move off into the shadow beside the stairwell. There was something about her, a toughness, perhaps; she wore some attitude he couldn't quite make out, something indefinite yet curiously old and familiar, too, and definite as a haze encircling her. Something Sarah had. The same thing. What?

"You'll catch your death in those wet things," she called from beside the telephone on the wall.

He looked down at his feet: true. A puddle had formed and he could see a slight steam rise softly from his pants legs.

Will the Addisons come home tonight or are they trapped in town? Stranded: absolutely, yes, the snowplows can't possibly start until morning. At the window he peered outside while Kate rang the ranch. Great snowflakes settled against the delicate etchings of frost on the glass; the skies brimmed.

He listened to Kate's explanations. They were at the Addisons', yes, and would be up as soon as Charlie something-or-other cleared the roads in the morning, but, no, it would probably be noon because there was a big snowslide, and, no, do nothing until Baskin gets there. Open some champagne. Over there in the shadow of the staircase, leaning against the wall and saying all this, she exposed a flash of brown leg.

A mere boy, eight years old when I left this place up here, he wanted to say, so you don't understand. You don't know that I left Sarah's innocent nudist colony and never came back all those awful summers of my puberty. This is nothing to you, an idle evening stranded down the road—it happens often up here, sure, everybody is always staying overnight unexpectedly with a neighbor—but here in the damp chill of this room I'm beginning to burn, to become incandescent. Kate talked on and on; in a patch of memory like a warm pool far back in his brain he recalled how she used to chat with Sarah back on Kimbark Avenue, dotting an ashtray with her cigarette stub, talking about books, perhaps, or reading aloud from the movie reviews or the gossip columns while he chased a lost symmetry of figures across that greenish kitchen blackboard not far off.

She's different now, he thought. Older, yes, but there's this new haze about her, this attitude. She gives off heat, but what sort? A deep burn, perhaps, and not just a warm sexual radiation.

I'm probably going to be conspicuous with my pants on, he decided, but what to do? She's still talking. I'm in my dark corner over here by the window and she's in her dark corner over there: polarized and naked, two pensive atoms whirling around a heady nucleus.

He made his way back to the fire, thinking: a sweet, intense slapstick, all this: Kate lingering on the telephone, fleshly speculations ambushing me. How did those men who came out here, those wayward, pale, silly businessmen, keep themselves unexcited when everyone was stripped for action on those erotic volleyball courts? Did they manage to keep it down and did Sarah, ever cunning, import Kate and such others to—what?—insure that everyone would keep coming back each year? The devices of loneliness are many. But did the men manage and how? Did they develop a sidestep, a sprightly cover-up, fingers zipping into place like a quick figleaf?

As the conversation on the phone closed, he sank down into the armchair. She came back to the hearth to stand beside him and report that everything was under control at the ranch, that everyone else had arrived, no problem, and for just an instant he caught sight of the robe falling away from her breasts before she tugged at it and closed off his view, and he was thinking, ah, don't look up, don't move.

"M-my thinking is based pretty much on numbers," he blurted out, disarming her, he supposed, with a *non-sequitur.* "I even remember the phone number at the ranch. I m-make lists in my head and usually number every single fact or piece of information I receive. For example, aside from my normal first impressions of you tonight—f-first physical impression, you know—I can probably recite to you the facts about yourself I've learned. Under your general file, see, I have these individual scraps of data."

He stared straight into the flames as he made this speech, not minding what Kate might make of it.

"The fourth thing I learned about you, say, is that you worked for some newspaper, a suburban newspaper, you said. Ah, each unit of information—I call the units *clusters* or, in current psychological jargon, *ch-chunks*—gets coded so I don't forget. The average person can remember, oh, ten or twelve consecutive numbers or units, but I can get thirty or so in my better days. My record is forty-one, as a m-matter of fact. But it's all a matter of training."

Kate was smiling down at him, he knew, but he didn't dare look up. The orange and yellow flame into which he had stared so long began to make his eyes water.

Now he was the one talking, talking on, his mind adream, of course, thinking: keep up the chatter, let her think I'm used to all this, to a nearly naked woman covering me in a tent of perfume, let her think I was raised cool and sophisticated up here, immune to all the pubic beauty Sarah placed around me.

Kate removed the boiling coffee and poured a cup for Baskin. Never mind the caves and meadows of that chenille, he repeated to himself, and he didn't look up.

"S-Sarah had all these learning gimmicks for me," he went on. "When she discovered that my real aptitude was for numbers she taught me to number everything—so my clusters began. At first I was conscious of n-numbering my clusters as I learned them, but not now. If someone asked what Number Six about Kate McCluskey was, I'd say, well, she had that solitary period in her life and got over her crisis."

A cold rivulet of water ran down his leg and he winced.

"That's a sort of impersonal way of learning about people, though, isn't it?" she asked.

She was doing something at the hearth, drinking her coffee, perhaps, or placing her undies over the grate to dry. Perhaps and perhaps: maybe she had let the robe fall away and stood there all naked, breasts enormous and commanding, waist delicate and hard, a creamy dear ass. Those delicate movements which he wouldn't acknowledge took his breath, his sense, his words.

"True," he managed at last. "But I don't really memorize people. It's just that I'm a cluster thinker and can't exactly stop." He seemed to be talking on now himself, filling up the room with his voice. All drivel. She puttered around the fireplace, seeming to plead for the gaze he wouldn't give.

She tossed a log on. He sipped his coffee noisily and kept jabbering. Saying what? He wasn't even listening to himself, thinking: we've both revived our whole personal histories these last silly hours and started a game of emotional hopscotch. Misery.

His frontside was blistering and his backside freezing so he got up, edged by her, head down, and went in search of old man Addison's clothes. Still talking, he noticed he had a full erection. The dark closet of that cold front bedroom was filled with all sorts of friendly woolens.

He talked. Even as he did he felt helplessly cast back into an old emotional contest—oh, those nerve-wracked competitions against which he had tried to insulate himself after leaving Sarah and Chicago. Now, he was telling himself, as he used to do, Kate has the advantage: I'm talking and she's listening, so I'm really on the defensive while she only has to stand there and be the strong silent one. An old fateful sort of reasoning took hold: life as hand-to-hand combat, love as open warfare, every minor conversation a terrible strategy and trial. Sarah's old way.

Kate was still at the hearth, diddling around. Unbearable. He made himself go back in there with her.

When he sat back down in his chair, she sat down on the rug beside him; her legs curled underneath, her bare knees shiny, her hair loose.

"I used to talk with Sarah about you, as you can probably imagine," she said warmly. He didn't know what to make of her sudden new tone. "Is speed all there is to genius, I mean? Can you just do things *faster*? Or do geniuses—I suppose you are one—have, well, *deeper* thoughts?"

It was generous of her, as if she wanted to give the advantage back to him now. He felt quieter, his heat cooling slightly.

"Oh, it's mostly speed," he could say, answering benevolently. He allowed himself to peek quickly down the folds of chenille at the soft beginning curves of her breasts, the tender brown slopes. "And memory," he added. "And also energy, I guess, and eccentricity and pride. You have to *want* to remember, though, and play all the necessary quick little games." He was falling into talking about himself, he knew, and, oh, he hadn't really ever done this, yet it was a comfortable enough feeling, almost enough to make him forget that he had reached a boiling point.

Then, after a while, he was talked out. "What time is it getting to be?" he asked her.

"Past two in the morning," she said drowsily, and she leaned over—oh, god—and placed her cheek down softly on his knee.

Quickthought: is this all that's going to happen now? Is she going to sleep?

Then, in the silence, he sat there in his usual summary, tired of his own voice and exhausted from his trip, reviewing the day, reciting clusters to himself—just as he had done since he was a child. I've learned, let's see, equations all indirectly related to the age of the universe (poor, poor cosmos), some information on western airline travel in the afternoon and evening, data on Kate all this long night: clusters everywhere.

The fire was low and beautiful.

He wondered, once more, how old Kate might be. Also: there's this familiar toughness about her. Sarah's legacy, definitely.

Then, toward morning, in spite of his fatigue, he sat there wide-eyed, Kate asleep on his knee, the fire all pale embers. The room had grown cold around them and he was looking down on her, feeling, somehow, his emotional adolescence lingering yet also ebbing away, the lessons of paradise beginning, his heart smashing along, and he reached down and softly touched her hair.

This is another course to take, he admitted. As usual, he supposed that once he had begun he would be precocious.

❧ V ❧

Noon the next day at the ranch. Dierker was there, firm of chin and hearty, a good sunlamp tan on his cheeks, with his usual entourage. Also present were Sarah's lawyer, Sarah's paperback publisher, a few of the old newspaper cronies, and the ranch hands—about twenty in all. The mood was relaxed and Dierker and his secretary (blond and girlish, Little Orphan Annie hairdo) mixed and served drinks. The conversation around the room, Baskin gratefully noticed, didn't stop when he and Kate made their appearance.

He shook hands all around. The room preoccupied him, though: that wide expanse of carpet where he played away whole winter afternoons with his model soldiers, the massive hearth with the stone like an owl's head, the oak desk with the old Royal typewriter, the windowseat where he and Sarah played Scrabble and five-minute chess, rows of familiar books along the shelves. Seeing it again, he felt a familiar pain and wonder. Dierker gave him a fatherly embrace. Odor of tobacco and vermouth. Kate removed her parka and stood there, wrinkled and disheveled, saying hello to everyone with him and it somehow made him feel comfortable.

There seemed to be lots to consider, so Baskin accepted a drink from the secretary and began. Swept with more nostalgia than he ever imagined he'd have, timid and slightly unsure of what haunted him in these old surroundings, he covered up as always by asserting himself. The lawyer, Max Neuborn from Kalispell, had the letter from Sarah which comprised her last will and testament. "It has all the funeral business in it, too," Neuborn reported, handing it over, and Baskin accepted it, nodded, and slipped it into the pocket of his suit jacket. One of the ranch hands stepped forward to ask if Baskin was hungry, and, yes, he wanted a bacon omelette—ask Miss Kate what she wants—and a few snacks, please, for those who were drinking. Then he gave the other men work, for which they seemed grateful. "I believe it's warming up outside and the snow might melt off a little this afternoon," he told them, "so you men look for a burial place up the hillside across the road. We want Miss Sarah where she wanted to be: in a spot that looks down on the property and the river."

The room, its familiar sensations: odors and images flew at him, but he kept talking, giving these friendly commands, and everyone seemed pleased to have him do it.

The secretary, Bennie, offered that they had the master bedroom fixed for him, but he said no, he preferred the loft. Could she make the switch? Kate came over, explained things to the secretary, then bounced her along to tend to it. One of the ranch hands stuck his head back inside the door.

"Want us to go ahead and dig, if h'it ain't too bad?" he wanted to know, and Baskin said yes and thanked him.

Slowly he began to feel that the room, these people, were giving off an old familiar warmth, a nearly forgotten security, and he thought of those windowless cubicles of his last years. To curl up in his old blanket beside the fire, to be caressed by the company of voices: ah, he felt he might just do that in time. Right now he went on distributing small duties like gifts. He chatted with Neuborn and DeMarco, Sarah's paperback publisher, and Kate was there reassuring him. Bennie came in, whispered in Kate's ear, and departed again. There was another girl, Tina, who was pretty and shy and seemed to belong to DeMarco, at least if Baskin read the exchange of smiles correctly.

In time, duty befell them. They went out to look at Sarah.

She lay on the back porch, shrouded in red. The glass panels were open, the wicker furniture had been set back against the walls, and it was like a refrigerator. Outside, though, the cloudbanks had parted and the sun slanted through; the day warmed, rivulets of melted snow would soon be trickling into the creeks, and Baskin suggested that they go ahead with the necessities that afternoon. They stayed only a moment.

Back inside food was laid out on the long table in the dining cove, everyone talked, drinks rattled, and Baskin felt slightly guilty for enjoying it all. The somber moments came, though, when different ones spoke to him about Sarah.

"I understand you didn't know about your mother's illness," Dierker said to him across the table once.

"You didn't know either," Kate put in. She smiled. "Almost no one knew."

Later Kate made another defensive move in Baskin's behalf. DeMarco had been talking aimlessly about Sarah and made a passing reference to Sarah's break with Baskin in Chicago.

"It was mostly her own fault and she admitted it herself," Kate said. "It was a matter of not quite letting go after all those years as his tutor."

Much more complicated than that, Baskin wanted to add, but he was grateful.

From the large bay window Baskin looked out beyond the river at the clouds hovering around the snowy edges of Mt. Kintla. The afternoon moved pleasantly. After eating his omelette he excused himself to read Sarah's letter and made his way toward the loft. En route, he met Tina, the shy girl, who was suddenly helpful.

"Can I get you anything?" she wanted to know. He decided against asking her if she was a secretary, too, like Bennie.

"Some tea, maybe," he told her. "When I come back downstairs I think a good cup of tea would do me."

Then he climbed up the hallway ladder to the loft. It seemed much smaller, the slant of the roof crowding him; the bed was narrow, one for a child who lived, long ago, in a story that took place in this house. Opening the drawer of his old desk, there they were—his baseball cards: Ernie Banks, Ralph Branca, Herb Score and the others. The afternoon games at Wrigley Field came to mind, the night games at Comiskey Park, Sarah with her can of beer. He sat beside her, engrossed, keeping the batting averages in his head and predicting plays. "Double steal," she said once, smirking. "What makes you think this will be a double steal coming up?" And there they went: Lou Brock leading the way, spikes flashing, the dash to home plate, a cloud of dust, cheers, the umpire's widespread arms. He shuffled through the pack of baseball cards now and thought: I never had anyone to trade these with, did I? Baseball cards, tokens of a hundred packs of bubble gum, these are, and you were supposed to exchange them with your neighborhood pals it said on the wrapper, but some things in life have to go undone.

He gazed out his window. Beyond the road, up on the hillside, he could see the men at work and the snow was darkened with an ugly mound of brownish dirt.

The letter wasn't addressed to him, but to Max Neuborn, but he gave the room an empty shrug and read it.

Sarah's familiar, jiggly handwriting; she was a good typist, but her scrawl was impossible.

Oh, Christ: she wants us to go to her funeral without our clothes on. Impossible.

Simple business and to the point *after that:* Sarah was leaving small amounts to the ranch hands and fifty thousand dollars to Kate McCluskey on the condition that Kate "remain at the ranch for one year, after which time she could possibly be of assistance to Baskin should he want to dispose of the property." Everything else, the ranch and lands, livestock, furnishings, and liquid assets —bonds, stocks, insurance policies, accounts, and future royalties from editions of the western novels—were left to Baskin. There was a condition, not exactly a legal one, and Baskin read it slowly.

Also, Max, I want you to ask Baskin if he won't please stay on at the ranch, too, for a period of one year from the date of my death. I don't want to make this a binding request, but it's the only thing I'm asking of him, so see if he won't do it. As things have turned out, I feel we owe each other something more, and I want this to be it. Of course you'll have to explain to him my commitments to Kate.

A year spent at the ranch: he read that part again, not sure of what he felt.

There were a few things more: mostly how she wanted her funeral conducted. Also, she asked that all present

59

pledges to her charities be extended for another year, that an estimated total of the value of the estate should be supplied Baskin as soon as possible, and that the letter be probated as previously arranged.

The whole thing was terse and impersonal and Baskin felt like an intruder. At the bottom of the last page, Neuborn had attached a brief estimate of the estate not including the ranch. It came to slightly over four hundred thousand dollars.

Baskin sat slumped on his narrow bed. He folded the letter back into the envelope and breathed a heavy sigh.

Later he asked Kate to select something to read at the graveside, something out of Sarah's own writing. It was a troublesome job because Sarah's style was short, tough, and action-packed. Kate said she could recall at least fourteen descriptions of various shoot-outs, but that she didn't believe they'd find anything poetic enough for the graveside.

"It's what she wanted. It's right there in the letter," Baskin said.

"What? Really?"

"She's trying her sense of humor on us again. That has to be it, but that's what she requested: a reading from her own works."

Kate gave him a hopeless look, but said she'd find something.

Baskin mingled again. Outside on the sundeck a definite warmth rode around in the air. April was the changeable month, he remembered, with snow and sudden gusts of warm air all in one day sometimes. Flood weather. It was now nearly three o'clock in the afternoon, over forty degrees, sunny, and the snow was melting away under the glare.

He glanced back through the bay window and saw

Kate surrounded by Dierker and three or four other men, and a tinge of jealousy pulsed around in him for a moment until he could say to himself: ah hell, this is silly. No reason to feel anything like that. Yet as he walked across the soggy road above the house he remembered—stupid, lovely image—the Addison place. Damn, think of something else.

The mass of a photon is equal to $h_\tau \div c^2$. Bus rides from the old U of Chicago along Lakeshore Drive, then up toward Wrigley Field. Old Professor Lothridge: I wonder if he would be sad at all this, if he would've come out here for our silly ceremony if he had known? Not many friends over the years, strictly speaking, that belong to me. Sarah's buddies, all these.

On the side of the hill above the road the ranch hands had finished their chore and Baskin stood there in the slush and mud duly complimenting them. "No real use waiting any longer either," he told them. "Let's bring Miss Sarah up here within the hour." Then he had the difficult job of inviting them to stay for the ceremony, yet explaining the delicacy of it all. Their boss and mistress, ah, that is, Miss Sarah, had asked for, well, a nude funeral. "You know how she was sometimes," he added hopefully.

"Naked?" one of the men asked for emphasis. The men gave each other a certain sly look.

"Of course you d-don't have to take part," he went on. "And if you do—ah, let's say the request is optional. It's a little chilly this afternoon and I suppose s-some of you have your own way of thinking about this sort of thing." Ridiculous saying it outright like this—even sillier than it looked written out in her letter—but Baskin went on with it, suffering a couple of tight grins. And, after all, the workers did know Sarah. Baskin only vaguely recalled there being ranch hands around when he was young, but there must have been; they must have always understood some things, surely.

He trudged back downhill to begin the unhappy business. Let Sarah have her last jokes, he decided. The whole matter began to amuse him slightly and he could see Kate reciting a gunfight scene or describing the pinto pony ridden by Tumbleweed Jack while all the ranch hands stood there, lean and salty, jeans and long-handle underwear in their arms, their bodies white with red stripes at the forearms and necks. He could envision Kate, Bennie, shy Tina, then, too, and his imagination tripped along. Then: I'm not taking my clothes off, bet on that. Request or no request.

Back inside the house he turned Sarah's letter over to Neuborn once more and asked him to read Sarah's instructions for the funeral to those gathered. It was to be announced that attire was optional.

The table in the cove was heaped with food again; the liquor supply dwindled, but everyone ate the food, stayed sober, and kept up a steady flow of reminiscences. Tina arrived with the cup of tea, then stood gazing at Baskin while he sipped, her own mouth silenced by large bites of cheese and bread. She wore her auburn hair long and combed straight. No stenographic talents, Baskin concluded as he sipped. When she talked, though, it was in a kind of hip shorthand. "Tea up," she told him as he let his lip dawdle at the rim of the cup, and when he asked her if she went to school in the East she said, "No, you smartee and me dropee." He didn't understand at first, but blinked and smiled.

Kate came to tell him that it was impossible to find anything appropriate in all those cowboy stories, but that, yes, she'd still try.

Then Dierker was making a toast, raising his glass and

saying, "To our sturdy girl," and it seemed right and everyone drank up and soon started up the hill.

As the letter also required, Baskin carried Sarah himself. She was just a small red bundle now, not the Sarah of pizzas and thick bologna sandwiches and strudel in the Chicago days, yet she was difficult to hold in all that wrapping. Besides, the path through the snow and slick mud to the grave was all uphill and treacherous. After about fifty yards, too, Baskin discovered that he wasn't used to the thin mountain air, so that by the time they reached the road he was gasping and wheezing. Then after a few more strides his right foot got caught in a suction of cold mud and wouldn't budge until one of the ranch hands came over to assist. The stuck shoe came off. The ranch hand held Sarah, supported Baskin while the shoe was replaced, and somewhat reluctantly gave her back. All this time the wind gathered in the pines and the sounds of the valley around them intensified, giving off a high descant to the procession.

Baskin imagined how it must look: a muddy, primitive troupe marching uphill, the weird bundle, Kate still fumbling those frayed paperback westerns, Little Orphan Bennie looking as though she were out for a nice hike, Dierker with a drink in hand and in seemingly good humor, shy Tina, the wildly expectant ranch hands and the somber business associates. What, he wondered, are the right emotions? As the slope increased he could hear his own rasping breath. What should we feel now? Painfully silly, all this, but maybe Sarah's greatest single work of art, this funeral: her first creation beyond cliché, a moment of serious comedy in which she finally catches and plays with her audience, makes them search themselves for their own feelings, surprises and entertains, pokes them with some paradox and jokes.

They arrived exhausted. Baskin decided to go ahead

63

and put Sarah in place instead of laying her down and hefting her again. Clumsily, then, assisted by two of the ranch hands, he slid off into the hole. His backside covered with cold slime, he fumbled to lay her out. Puddles of muddy ice in the bottom of the hole edged into his shoes.

"Okay, Mama," he told her. "Here you are. Just like in the letter: all natural."

He rested. Pausing to get his breath, he listened to the rising wind off in the distant pines. The mountains rose up all white and lovely in the distance, and, yes, this is a good place, he told himself, just as Sarah used to describe it: gaudy pretty.

Then he couldn't get out. The sides of the grave were slick and cold and the men couldn't give him a hand without sliding off into the opening themselves. Baskin struggled up on one elbow, slipped, tried again. Thick mud covered him. At last someone reached him with the handle of a shovel and pulled him up.

There he stood, coated with mud, breathless, but just in time to see shy Tina open her topcoat and let it fall away. She was magnificently naked and Baskin looked away, looked back, and looked away again at the poor ranch hands who stood there hypnotized with the sight of her. Both Bennie and Kate were taking off their clothes, too. Bennie got undressed first, almost as effortlessly as Tina: long willowy girl's body with small breasts, all blond, that mop of curls topping her off. Kate removed her things slowly, stacking them neatly atop the piled snow. She had several books with the pages marked and fumbled those around and it seemed forever until she was ready. She was an unusually handsome woman, no denying it. Baskin wondered again how old she was; not old at all, judging by that shape, but her eyes and mouth were accented with crow's feet. Heavy breasts, a little over-large, but a flat stomach and strong brown legs. Too much. Then Dierker: he was the only man to comply— probably because of his proud sunlamp tan. There he stood with his chin upright, his worsteds in his arms, trying to look casual while the ranch hands gawked and Kate began her reading. Bennie's poor nipples turned hard as pebbles; across from her, stupefied, all the cowboy jaws had stopped working tobacco.

The first passage was the only good one, something about the mountains, lovely killers, sitting serene and cold. Then Kate was trying a passage about a gunfighter considering his last night on earth. It didn't work at all and Baskin found himself grinning slightly. Also, as he concentrated on the words, his eyes wandered away.

Once as he looked at Kate she returned his gaze and he had to look elsewhere. She was simply splendid, of course, just too much, yet now it wasn't last night's healthy lust he felt but a kind of helpless tender regard. For one thing, she was cold and he saw her shiver slightly, but also the naked body has a vulnerable, childish look to it; she seemed very alone, very small, standing there in the great outdoors. He smiled at her efforts.

Sarah and all those long ago summers: he couldn't help thinking of them. Down there at the river he had gathered colored stones, set them off in separate piles and graded them; geology lessons along the steep cliffs where the river bends. They built a waterwheel together: his early lessons in hydrodynamics. All the creatures of his biology lessons, too: everything from water mites to grayling to that bleached skeleton of the beaver which they found on the far shore. Naked and bouncy, wearing only her tennis shoes, Sarah led their expeditions. Because of the mosquitoes they always smelled strongly of citronella and at age six, in fact, Baskin worried about it; he thought he might stumble, slip off into the river, and float all the way to the Polebridge Store—oily and buoyant, yes, but terrified and unable to get to shore—before they could rescue him.

Sarah: good-bye now, Mama.

Kate's pages flapped in the rising breeze, but she went on searching out phrases and passages. Once she read on past a paragraph she had marked and smiled to herself—it must have been wretched prose. Then, at the end, she couldn't keep the bargain and read a psalm or two. A really sexy woman, a real winger, Baskin concluded, and he noticed that in spite of Tina's extraordinary young figure and Bennie's sweet curves the gaze of all those middle-aged ranch hands had settled on Kate. Her voice strained in the noisy wind, but was full and honeyed.

Then Baskin was watching his father. Old Dierker was the same as ever: a man dedicated fully to the moment, an ingenious inventor of games and the creator of recreations. It seemed to Baskin that he ought somehow to see himself reflected in that tanned optimism and strong jut of chin, but he didn't. Dierker had passed along some good strong genes, nothing much more. If Sarah was industrious, Dierker was naturally lazy; his only bursts of energy came when there was fun to be had—or so it seemed. Baskin stood there wishing there were something they could say to each other on such an occasion.

Now DeMarco and his Tina, Jack Neuborn and Bennie were all sniffling. The psalm reading did it. Sarah, you didn't want that, right, but you never get it like you want it. I'm not even in the buff for you, am I? My sweater and seersuckers are caked with Flathead mud and Kate has found your prose wanting.

Then it was over.

The girls and Dierker dressed haphazardly.

On the way back down, Kate caught up with Baskin and took his hand.

At the party that night he began thinking, ah, well, it was a nice enough funeral. Feeling slightly guilty for not having undressed and worked things out in strict compliance with Sarah's wishes, he decided that he would have to do the one thing she had requested: he'd stay on at the ranch. Where was there to go? He was tired of the work he was doing, that sensational rote work for which everyone overpraised him, and he had been feeling the approach of a great unrest with himself, after all, one of those emotional low tides he didn't want to suffer. Breakdowns are too melodramatic, he told himself, and I'm above them, and, sure, I'll just stay here.

The old crowd sang while Kate played the guitar. Outside, the night air had frozen the melting snow again, stopping the rivulets in their paths, and in the morning, he knew, it would be warm again and sun would fill up the valley. He sang with everyone else in his off-key tone. The song evolved into "My Darling Clementine."

❧ VI ❧

The hours and days would begin to pass along at a slow new pace now, and in the mornings, wrapped in an old familiar ballast of heavy quilts and blankets up there in his loft, Baskin would start to remember again. Memory: his art and curse. It would come at him gently sometimes, rich with pleasant good thoughts, then at other times it would turn on him and he'd recall one of those nearly forgotten seasons of shouts and intimidations and silly fights that occupied him and Sarah back in Chicago. Or, passing through the main room he'd catch sight of the Scrabble set or the dusty microscope or a broken fountain pen—the one she used to write *Santa Fe Shoot Out*—idling on the desk. Or, outdoors, he'd toss up some very old clusters of his and let them fall through his head, re-creating the apartment they had near the Fermi Institute, the snow around the campus, his first cup of coffee at age twelve, all those plays and ballets where Sarah pumped him full of information the whole time so that he couldn't ever really enjoy any of it, packing him full of culture just as she packed him full of life and lessons.

It was four days after the funeral before Dierker finally

left the ranch, but his staying on failed to interrupt Baskin; the reveries began. For one thing, Dierker was always out of the way playing. After everyone else departed Dierker pulled out the flyrods and fished the river; then he went up Tepee Creek (four small native trout, a bruised ankle), then up Hay Creek (ten trout this time, but a bruise on top of the bruise and a whelp on his nose), and when he was tired of fishing he and the ranch hands—who lingered to be paid their winter wages before going off, as usual, to help on farms outside the valley—devised some entertainments. One was some sharpshooting inspired by Dierker's purchase at the Polebridge Store of a case of aerosol shaving cream dispensers. Down to the meadow went all the men except Baskin, resourceful Dierker leading the way, box of shaving cream cans aloft, to take a few shots with a couple of .22 pistols found among Sarah's clutter at her reading chair in the library. Since all these old cowboys and Dierker himself were good shots, they zapped the cans at distances up to seventy-five yards and the meadow bloomed with strange mushrooms whiter than the snow, lime and menthol flavored, and the men howled and congratulated each other on the effects. Pop: a dull explosion, a geyser of lather, another mushroom. Later, when the sun came out the piles of shaving cream became airy and porous and evaporated into the clear Flathead afternoon with the surrounding snow.

On Dierker's last night Kate prepared dinner and they were talking along—Baskin wasn't paying too much attention—and Dierker said, "You know how I'm going to die? Listen, now, a prophecy: I'll get myself killed in an amusement park. Disneyland or Six Flags Over Texas or Santa's Village: one of our really big amusement parks somewhere. It'll be during my second, maybe third, childhood. Say, on some parachute jump—with my strings tangled up."

Baskin and Kate gave him smiles.

"Amusement is a destructive force, let me tell you, but it's still amusement! Work is *always* killing. A sure thing. I've seen New York too long and I know."

"You *will* go back to work now, though, won't you?" Kate asked, her lips pursed.

"Right. But I'm enjoying myself down to the last and you can't blame me for it. Sarah—so to speak—still provides." He laughed, thoughtfully, and forked in a bite of potato. "So I enjoy the mountains. Enjoy the snow on the aspens. Enjoy you in your blue jeans and good Baskin here brooding around the place."

A gentle criticism. Baskin took it and smiled into his food. Quickthought: by radiation measurement we know the movement of the earth, the speed of the galaxy, that there exists a distant sea of radiation. Who am I? What am I doing here? He couldn't get with it, couldn't converse. After supper they went in beside the fire where Dierker's wit came flying at them; it had that slightly off-center strain to it, an undercurrent of effort suffered by a man who had to try hard to bend the talk his way. But Baskin listened to his father pronounce and comment.

On literature as they talked about his job: "No, I'm not literary. That is, I don't possess a long list of big books that only I have read."

On pornography in the same conversation: "A dirty mind makes solitude so much more enjoyable."

On himself, later: "Some people think I'm an intelligent editor, yes. I'm not so sure, but I can't argue with their line of reasoning."

On life, somewhat ambiguously: "Either you sniff the same old rose or you get a variety of shit."

On Sarah's career: "She told me once that since she was a hack writer she was always at her best."

Advice (fatherly) to whom it may concern: "From my observations around here, I'd say one thing about you, Baskin: you're going to have to work very hard at being natural."

To Kate with a grin: "Oh, I know you never have much liked me, but of course every time I ask you to shed a little light on our problems with each other you flare your temper."

Once during all this Baskin dutifully offered a description of exactly what he did in the lab at New Orleans. Mathematical chemistry, yes. Difficult to explain. Dierker prodded him, so for a moment he listened to the sound of his own voice, realizing that he couldn't talk to his father because, perhaps, there were too many important things to say that couldn't be uttered. He liked Dierker all right, but there it was: they would never talk on any other frequency than this. Besides, Dierker, as always, was having a love affair—unassisted.

At the end of those four extra days Baskin drove Dierker down to Kalispell in the Jeep. In the silence between them, Baskin composed equations in his head and ruminated on some of the problems he had left in his cubicle in New Orleans. At the airport, though, waiting for the ground crew to roll out the little Stinson that would fly Dierker over the mountains to his connecting flight at Great Falls, his father turned to him and said, "Well, I'm coming back out—maybe late summer. Is that all right with you?" And Baskin said yes, sure, and they took a long look at each other, searching around in the eyes, maybe, for some similar glint, something mutual and comprehensible, and for a moment Baskin wondered if they were going to shake hands or not. They didn't. But the plane didn't get ready either and they were standing out in a cold wind, so they finally went inside. There, beside a hulking coffee machine at the rear of the one-room depot, Dierker asked for a loan.

"Don't really have to have it for a couple of weeks," he said awkwardly. "And not even then, if you can't swing it. But it's a personal thing: money I've spent, if you want to know, that my family needn't know about."

"No problem," Baskin assured him. "But I'll have to locate all the accounts, I guess, so it will take a few days."

"You can just mail it to my firm."

"No problem."

"I'll get it back to you before summer."

"No problem," Baskin kept repeating. Then: "How much do you need?"

"Two thousand," Dierker said. "I'll get it back before summer, but it's a small problem now."

Driving back up the Flathead valley, Baskin consoled himself with the thought that, well, it was two thousand dollars, after all, that Dierker managed for Sarah on those first pulp novels. The circle has just come full round. Then he was thinking about Sarah's writing habits, how she glided around the room as she concocted adventures for her Sam Quick, Red Rayder, Amarillo Kid and assorted roughriders. First she'd stand at the mantel, poking up the fire as she read over her previous day's work, then she'd switch to the reading chair to pencil out a rough draft of some new ambush or chase, then she'd go over to the good Royal typewriter to fill up five or six pages of yellow paper with spelling errors (a lapse from her reporting days when she took care with all such details) and terse dialogue and clichés. All during this, of course, she'd fire off glances at her chubby son playing on the floor or lying in a tangle of his own arms and legs with a book in the velvet seat of the bay window. Sarah's work: an American Dream capitalized upon: the loner against nature, odds, old grudges, frantic savages, the greed for gold, the closed range. Somehow, surely, the real Sarah dreamed apart from all that.

And where did the real Dierker dream? Two thousand dollars. A curious sum, considering Dierker's probable annual income. An unexpected turn of events, too. Is it just that he made this trip on the sly, Baskin wondered, so that he needs some cash to explain a hole in his bank account to his wife, as he said? Or are there some dark corners in happy daddy? I'm not good with people; they're sums greater and stranger than their various small parts and never add up. Yet the questions come: who are they? what lives did they live? what changes waylaid them? The little, gossipy, petty, awful, cosmic questions: integers which form the constellation, the cluster that is me.

To think on oneself—whether in a moment of idle vanity or in the philosophic void of existential seriousness—was useless bad taste. A waste, an indulgence, and, well, unmanly, because life—and Baskin still believed what Sarah had preached about this, at least—was best lived at the arrowpoint of intelligent action, and, yes, there would be mistakes and foolishness, indeed, but the bog of regrets and guilt and self-evaluations and self-inflicted ideologies and posturing was to be sternly avoided. Though I feel the encroachment of change, then, he could say to himself, I want to think as an actionist and not as some mewing melancholy initiate.

The old Northfork Road soared underneath him; icicles, catching the afternoon rays, winked among the pine and aspen.

Think on things to do: Sarah's clutter to be sorted, wood to be chopped, tag ends of business and accounts, a check for Dierker. Think on Kate and the dream of dreams: seduction. Down there at the airport in that first moment her eyes were flashing messages. Weren't they? Her figure straining at that chenille robe, oh, that unbelievable night. Right out of a thousand class-B movies, out of a familiar party joke, out of my primordial adolescent fantasy! Her hand on mine coming downhill from that sloppy sad funeral. Her slow shuffling in the house below me at night when I'm tucked away like Little Boy Blue in the loft. What does she do? Comb out her hair? Rub creams into that torso, those thighs? Parade her incredible ass into the kitchen?

Think on ways to go about it. Direct approaches: an unembarrassed erection. A vulgar and vivid proposition. Or just the casual approach: "Ah, Kate, this morning's wood chopping has given me a nasty backache, so would you mind rubbing in this liniment? Here, let me drop my sleeve off." Also my shirt, blue jeans, underwear, and this flesh beyond my flesh, this bone, this marrow, these tender atoms whirling around my soul. In the moonlight there she lies, open like a nightflower, reeking with the honeyed pollen of sex. Think on the curvature of space, think on the nature of time, think on, think about something else.

❧ VII ❦

―――――――――

But there was little else to ponder except Kate. She continued to shuffle beneath his floor in the insomniac night and sway through his days in that smooth denim walk of hers.

He studied her. Although they managed no really personal conversations those next days, he began to analyze that somehow familiar mood about her, that small yet detectable source of her; it had been Sarah's, that mood, but he had never really been old enough to understand it exactly and now here it was again. Only one word for it, he knew: bitterness. It surrounded her like a haze, sat in the fall of her mouth, passed over her eyes. Life had handled her and she was in retreat and vengeful, yet, at the same time, curiously open, still sexual, still alive, so that the cynicism had not blown out the deepest fuse in her. Sometimes he decided that he thought about her too much, but there she was occupying his dreams and awakenings.

For one thing she made no pretense to move back out to her former rooms at the new bunkhouse alongside the river. "So much needs tending to," she kept complaining as she emptied out all the drawers and bureaus and closets of Baskin's remembrance. For more than a week they inspected faded yellow notes, trinkets, trash, old letters. At times he found himself at her side and he would catch a breath of her perfume—she doesn't wear that perfume for herself alone, he decided—and he would stammer and cough and pay elaborate attention to the object at hand and wonder if she wondered about him. At night his insomnia waylaid him and he would go into the reading room and piddle at Sarah's accounts or tune in the short-wave radio for weather reports from Great Falls, Juneau, or Seattle. In those prolonged hours—he missed his lovely eight-hour dreamless sleep every night—he'd try to imagine how he could find an excuse to go to her room, to appear in lustful silhouette at her door, to invite himself slyly to the side of her bed. They'd remember something funny and laugh together, he'd make puns, she'd grow lighthearted, tipsy with laughter, her head thrown back, brown breast partially exposed as the coverlet slipped away from her nightgown, ha ha, laughing hilariously, his hand falling good-naturedly on her leg, oh my, tilting and falling toward each other in ever-so-slight convulsions, ho ho, spasms of giggles turning them weak and giddy, ha, and he'd be easing her panties down, her brown shoulders bumping with delight as she couldn't stop laughing, ha, and another sweet pun, a play on words, ho, and in he'd go.

The forecast was for dreary snow through the first part of the new month of May, according to the man on the shortwave. Where was this forecast for? Alaska? Somewhere nearby? Baskin stared around the main room longing to hear Kate's voice calling him above the drone of the set. Two prints by the artist Charles M. Russell stared back at him from across the room: "Lewis and Clark Meeting the Flatheads" near the bay window and "Discovery of Last Chance Gulch" near the front door: cowboys and indians forever, the world when it was wonderfully simple. For several evenings he allowed his gaze to set on those detailed illustrations, Sarah's favorites, while thinking how he might start a really bawdy conversation with Kate. At least something lightly intimate: how he and Sarah used to take baths in the old wooden tub right there in front of the fireplace, how the hearth became a slippery marsh, bar of soap sliding under the couch, and, oh, the fun of it and how about giving it a try with me, ha ha, just peel off right here, I'll get the tub, just peel for a replay of that scene at the Addison place, please, rub-a-dub-dub?

Where does the lonely mind travel? Ah, let me tell you, Kate. In Manhattan, on Kimbark Avenue, or in Audubon Park the mind's assorted reels of simple lust travel faster than light (186,000 miles per second) and they break and flap in the head and cut the brain, and, oh, I would have given one hundred points of my acclaimed IQ for one small communication at times, one simple coffee break, say, with some nincompoop secretary tugging at the hem of her skirt or one stroll with some old-fashioned hand-holding or one simple doorway kiss. Kate, imagine one of my really brilliant fantasies, one of my gleaming pornographic productions of the inner eye, a vivid image from my solitary nightbed, my waste. That little waitress stretching to serve my birthday cake, that coed ambling toward me on the walkway near St. Charles Place, that busty librarian: small photographs kept and stored away forever.

The weatherman droned on. A long-range forecast for a sudden thaw and a warm late spring.

So went the night and nights after that.

It was later, toward the middle of May, that they

started having talks. They would be out tending the horses or driving down to Kalispell for groceries and there would be those brief illuminations, Kate saying something of sudden importance.

"Either you beat the men or get beaten by them," she said one day, for instance, as they were working out in the vegetable garden. It came out as they were talking about Sarah's business sense.

"That's a competitive thing to say," Baskin told her. He leaned on his hoe. As she knelt there was a lovely stretch of denim across her inner thigh.

"Well, I'm a competitor. Don't let this fool you, my being up here out of things just now."

A high wind skimmed the tops of the hovering mountains. Baskin could feel the heat of the sun on his neck and shoulders and the cold rising from the ground beneath him.

"Was Sarah competitive?" Baskin asked.

"What do you think her writing was about? She loved getting paid for writing what she did. It was her way of getting at publishing, at the money game that conspired against her, at the stupid male ego that fed on her cowboy stories, and everything else."

She never looked up, just kept popping seeds into the ground, and he went inside after a while and thought about what she said about Sarah and, yes, naturally that's why she wrote those stories, of course, hearing it said outright like that made it so perfectly clear. And it came to him that in spite of all he knew about Sarah—her drives, her moods, her ambition for him, all her vitalities—he probably only knew her through the fog of his childhood remembrances and probably not very well at all.

Quickthought: Sarah found some of my crude sketches of naked women once in Chicago and flushed them down the toilet. Unlike her.

So he would remember again, drift into reveries, weigh things out. Between Kate's presence and Sarah's memory the days swung along.

"You were one of Sarah's weapons against the world, you know," Kate said another time. "She tried to prove with you that she didn't need anyone and that she could be a university all by herself."

"It didn't work, though," Baskin answered.

"No, the project got out of hand. The project had a mind of its own, so it got out of hand. But that was the way it was once, isn't that right?"

"That's exactly it," Baskin said.

Exactly. When Sarah brought him to the University of Chicago she expected to remain in control and for some weeks and months she was a part of every experiment and phase of his work. The good doctors asked her to conferences, took her to lunch over at Mandel Hall, ushered her behind the two-way mirror while Baskin quipped and laughed and performed his small miracles for their colleagues. At night, too, it was mother and child: he curled into that firm hollow between her arm and breast with tender frequency as they read Mallory, Melville, Robert Louis Stevenson, Arthur Conan Doyle, Mark Twain and all the other basics. Or, if they were in a rowdy mood, it was off to Comiskey Park for double plays and double hot dogs ("We have to limit ourselves tonight, hon. We're getting so goddamned chubby!") and the crush of the crowd.

Then, later, as Kate knew, it was different. He was ten years old, wearing the long gray-striped trousers bought at Marshall Field's he liked so much, and they were just outside Dr. Ludmiller's office yelling at each other. *Sarah:* "Why shouldn't he be proud of you? You're doing tricks I taught you! All the shortcuts—they're mine! They're what makes him think you're a mastermind!" *Little Boy:* "But

what I know is in *my* head! It belongs to *me* now!" *Sarah:*
"Selfish!" *Little Boy:* "Let me pick *his* head! Let me find
out what he can teach me, Mama!" *Sarah:* "I can do it better, though! Don't bother with this course, Baskin, believe
me, it's a loser!" *Little Boy:* "He's a Doctor of Philosophy
in Math! This is the University!" *Sarah:* "I can do it better! When have I ever not done it better, come right
down to it?" *Little Boy:* "Mama! I just don't believe you!
Sorry!" And of course what he didn't know at the time,
he now understood, was that the problems and techniques which Ludmiller and the others poured into his
baby skull could be learned by almost any decent mathematician, Sarah included, and that he was only remarkable because he was a prodigy, a lad with striped pants
and chocolate on his sleeve and a modest grin. And what
he didn't know—*couldn't* possibly—was Sarah the woman,
Sarah the solitaire. He could only sit there in the shadows of the mountains now, ten years older, and grope
awkwardly backward and realize that she had accomplished all that he had done, had read all the same texts,
figured the same equations, and that apart from those
gritty tasks she had lived more fully than he had ever
dreamed.

Image: Sarah coming into the apartment, leaning back
against the closed door, biting her lip, eyes puffy with
tears. Another date gone wrong. She tried men and they
tried her occasionally, but her heart obviously beat a
strange and different rhythm. Was it Dierker wrecking
her love life? Did she needle her innocent dates like she
did me? Drive them to better themselves? Or did she
rape them and break them, eat and devour them? Who
was my mother in Chicago?

Deep in such considerations Baskin tended the chores
around the ranch house and tried to get his soft body to

respond to the wilderness. The ranch hands had delivered wood to the pile, but it still needed chopping and stacking, so he went at that. The axe head flew off into the woods and he spent half of one morning searching for it in a lovely tangle of poison ivy. Back at work the next day, a chip flew up and cut his cheek. He built up one nice evening blaze in the big hearth and forgot to open the flue. Worst of all, the new activity, far from trimming off weight, made him ravenous and he gorged nightly on Kate's big meal.

By June, then, he was slightly overweight, constantly scratching, dying for Kate's touch, lost in recollection of Sarah, out of sorts. He decided to take a pack trip over the mountain into Quartz Lake, a fishing trip not as Dierker might do it with all the comforts of an indoor picnic, but as a purge. I'll at least substitute total physical torture for this lingering sexual ordeal, he told himself, and so he packed a bedroll, gear, fishing equipment, food, and announced his plan to Kate.

"How heavy is that pack?" she asked, pointing.

"I haven't weighed it."

"Can you pick it up?"

"Sure, I think so."

Smiling, she got down Sarah's old maps of the high country and found that he would be climbing seven miles up and then walking five miles down into Quartz Lake. A steady smirk began to fix itself on her face as she offered a few suggestions about his baggage.

"These canned goods will have to stay—that first of all," she said.

"Right," he said. Then, innocently: "I'm going to get a fresh start first thing in the morning."

She was laughing, then, and he thought to himself, ah, here's a nice chance to give her a nice guffaw and hug, to establish a small breakthrough, but she turned and walked off, going down the hallway, laughing her deep laugh, lovely ass asway, giving him that amused womanly condescension as he stood there with the big cans of peaches and beans stacked neatly beside his walking boots.

⊰ VIII ⊱

He drove the Jeep down to the Polebridge Store early the next morning just as Cone, the storekeeper, opened for the day. Inside he breathed the strong odors of pine oil and open cheeses and surveyed the tall shelves of red soup cans. As Cone and his neighbor, Ossinger, an old German, played their first morning game of checkers beside the potbellied stove in the back room, Baskin ate a breakfast of Vienna sausages, crackers, cheese and milk. Cone brought him a cup of coffee, offered his condolences about Sarah, and sold him an assortment of dry trout flies. It was a warm store, comfortable, modest, the only outpost in thirty miles except for the cluster of ranger cabins across the river and the fire lookout up Hay Creek road. Once, when Sarah first came to this country, the store was the last civilization for an even greater distance, but the encroachment of the dutiful rangers and the inevitable tourists and absentee owners—people who had built new summer places—had brought a meager population. Cone seemed less a man of the frontier, as the boy Baskin once viewed him, than just another small businessman, and sitting there now Baskin could think, well, soon the valley will be crisscrossed by happy trails, tourists skipping along with their packages, and the banks of the rivers and lakes will be lined with expectant faces, the glaciers will be melted away, the stars will be captured, the world will be all paved.

At the ranger's cabin Baskin stopped for a fire permit. He had walked only half a mile from the Polebridge Store—down a strip of rock-strewn road and across the bridge—and already his pack straps cut into his shoulders so that he dreaded picking up his load after the courtesies with the ranger were finished. But he started out: up the road toward Bowman Lake, then across the ridge into Quartz, the middle and smallest of a chain of three lakes, actually, where he would camp. A steep climb all the way.

His load dizzied him after five hundred yards. He sat on a rock, unwilling to take it off his back because he knew he might not get it back on. High winds in the tamaracks. Sound of water everywhere: the snows melting in these first days of June, the ancient springs pouring, the creeks booming white and treacherous, the river far below echoing from ridge to ridge. He listened to the sounds of his own body, too: the protest of his breath, a furious heart.

At noon, above Bowman Lake on the ridge, he fell asleep in the elastic cushion of pine needles beside the trail, a trail nearly obscured in places by this new season's new growth. Later, he awoke to a crackling in the brush. A bear? An angry elk? Then he struggled into harness again, fixing his gloves under the shoulder straps this time to ease the bite.

Who was my mother in such a country as this? In Chicago she was worn with the city's gray erosion, all mussed with the harassment of apartment living, argumentative, frustrated, bent with her loneliness and horny for a man; out here she gained her solitude—dear kind word—and she contended that all this wild beauty sustained her, yet what did she really feel? In such brutal nature, perhaps, she could do battle; she could be stoic, hard, self-reliant against this raw life whereas Chicago was always complex. The professors made her anxious and I tormented her. The thing she built, me, slipped out of her control like a book gone bad in an author's hands.

You never climbed like this, did you, Mama? You never tried the mountains hand to hand, alone.

His lips began to quiver and he could feel his body grow weak, so that he had to sit down again. He seemed to be shaky with hunger although he had climbed scarcely an hour since lunch and he cut off a piece of summer sausage and ate it. The river, far below now, curved and glistened through the filter of trees; though it was early afternoon the grass was jeweled with dew, softly flashing, and everything around him seemed alive so that he began to listen. Grouse, squirrel, chipmunk, hawk, insects: each signaled, registered down deep in his awareness like small pulses of new knowledge. Thirty minutes passed, then he got up.

At the summit of the ridge he paused again, staggered under his pack, then started down. Wildflowers gilded the path now and his pack bumped his backside in rhythm as he went; he could feel exhaustion setting in and it rankled him. Where has my strength gone? I've got to live the physical life, he said to himself dumbly. Then he thought of Kate's soft brown mound, her thicksoft breasts and narrow waist. To have her with me out here, oh: carrying half my load, if nothing else. Kate, you're my private pornograph.

Glimmer of lake. Descending, the cool air pressed on

his face and he could feel the dampness rising from the shadowed fern and flowers along the path. A tree lay across his way and he tried to hurry over it, but tangled, stumbled, and took a fall; hurt more than he wanted to admit, he went on.

At the lakeside he shucked off his pack and sat for a while on a long log that extended out over the water. The lake and sky were mirrors held up against his life and he watched a golden eagle turn, glide, swoop beyond the far shore. Dusk came suddenly and he was too tired to think of eating anything, so he curled into his bedroll; later, deep into the night, he awoke in a bath of stars and lay there looking up, through the edge of the Milky Way, beyond the cold hush of space.

Then morning. He edged along the bank for a few yards—oh, misery in my knees from the climb, in my chest from that tumble—and took a trout, easily, on the second clumsy cast. The fire felt good, then, in the early chill and he had fried fish, fried bread, jam and coffee.

Cluster: the flowers and plants I remember are the glacier lily, beargrass, indian paintbrush, common perennial gaillardia or brown-eyed-susan, American falsehellebore, western pasqueflower, Sitka mountain-ash, fireweed, aster and aspen fleabanes, bearberry honeysuckle, common cowparsnip, red baneberry, western thimbleberry and, oh, Sarah, lessons are still coming out of my ears. You loved me into learning, sure, and when that didn't work you badgered and prodded me and when that didn't work you tried to shame me and when that didn't work you went hysterical then loved me again and told me how magnificent I was, how I could be pure mind, and I recall standing out on that promontory above Wedge Canyon where we spotted the wolverine, all proud, and you said, "Watch him, honey, and see how he moves. He

86

walks full of caution, see, because he's a vanishing species and he knows he has to be careful."

Cluster: there are uncommon beasts in our forest, yes, the wolverine walking in the knowledge of his extinction, the marten, an occasional grizzly bear ambling around all inquisitive, and the lemming. And birds: the eagle gold and bald, the osprey, Clark's nutcracker, the water ouzel, a thousand thrushes and warblers. Memory wheels them in front of my eyes and I see them like detailed drawings in my wildlife book or in that sudden first sighting when I saw them alive, Sarah pointing her stubby finger, saying, "There!"

By midday he had strolled around half of the small lake. His flyline split the water occasionally, lay still, twitched, then wrenched straight with a trout. He took nine fish, keeping three for his next meal, all small, and the snow on the mountains just above him caught the sun and warmed him. At the mouth of the creek that poured in from the upper, larger lake he fought a big one—under a rock, out, a frenzy of top water, a dive beneath that same rock—until he finally lost it. Somehow he felt glad about it and went on.

Quartz Creek: somewhere near here, he recalled, there was a copper strike and a rush of prospectors, the whole area filling with madmen from downworld, the Blackfeet indians pushed out, bought off. And long before that what passed this way? Trappers and isolatoes, desperate men each one, cut off from their various societies as I— oh, maudlin overstatement, perhaps—am cut off from mine. How did I remember the copper ore? Something else Sarah pumped into me, perhaps, but we never came this way. And this lost area of Glacier Park goes beyond all that, of course, all the way back to extinct species of bison and stone arrowheads and pre-history. Time laps us. I wonder about ghosts: does something inhabit this ground I tread? some essence of a man gone to cinder and dust who feels me in his place and transmits to me? or was that old trout I lost an ancestor of another whopper, instilled with a strange primordial sense and preknowledge?

He found himself in a tangle of fallen juniper and lodgepole pine, broken limbs assaulting him, and as he tried to keep his flyrod free he could feel a stab of pain from the day before in his ribs. Then, as he straddled one of the fallen trees, the brush rumbled ahead of him.

Sprack! A limb split and he saw it: a giant brown bear rousing itself.

He was watching it, gently easing himself backward now over the same tree trunk, when the bear stood, raising itself to an immense height, posing, menacing, jaw agape. Baskin could feel his neck tighten, his eyes bulge, and he went back, back, slowly crossing the wreckage of timber, angling around limbs which pricked like stakes. If the bear hadn't made a noise perhaps Baskin wouldn't have fallen, but there it came: a loud, disgruntled sigh, and over Baskin went, down between the slant of timbers with a crash. His terror was too great for him to be hurt just then, but the bear suddenly moved off in a crouching run up the side of the hill.

There. That does it, he admitted. I'm the clumsiest. His shin had caught a protruding branch on the way down and pulsed with pain, his flyrod was snapped in half like a twig, his face bled from a scratch, his breath was gone, his pride, his senses and he remembered, yes, spilling wine on the tablecloth at the faculty lounge in New Orleans, stumbling across trolley tracks, missing curbs and falling, the whole history of his awkwardness. I've got to learn to walk in the world, he told himself stupidly, I've just got to.

The leg wasn't broken, but hurt so badly that he didn't want to look at it. Moving deliberately, he gathered up the two sad pieces of his flyrod and his fish whose scales were scraped and dappled with pine dust. His pants had been torn with the impact and around the frayed edges of the hole he saw—only a quick glance, please—a dark red seepage.

His camp seemed too distant, beyond the creek and around the lake. Half a mile, more. He limped down to the water's edge and made his way along.

Later, at dusk of this second day, after another long nap—his eyes grew heavy at this altitude and he always seemed just a half breath short—he awoke to find a tower of black cloud edging over the ridge. Gathering his gear, unfolding his slicker hastily, he placed everything back under the thickest stand of pine and covered it; then he hobbled around gathering dry wood and starting his evening fire. When finished, he sat down finally and had a look at his leg; there wasn't much blood, but the blow had cut down to the bone and there were two large purple rolls of skin. No first aid kit. Bandages, what for bandages? He tore up his undershirt and wrapped the wound lightly, mainly for protection, then started his supper, wishing for one of those big cans of fruit Kate had rightly instructed him to leave behind.

Just after dark he lay in his bedroll, covered with the slicker, as it began to rain. The whole animal kingdom seemed to be scurrying for cover around him.

Eugene Marais' account of the two African baboons who leapt from a cliff onto the back of a leopard about to attack their group, killing both themselves and the attacker. The adult homosexual relationships between apes, elephants, porpoises, giraffes; complete marital fidelity among wolves, swans, foxes, and others. The *Australopithecus africanus*. The animal is wiser than scientists have ever guessed, Sarah once mused, and probably capable of symbolic reasoning, abstract thought, language, perhaps even poetry. He lay there in the deafening drizzle thinking all this, wondering if the seasoned creatures who peered out of the undergrowth at him didn't think about how foolish he was. Wild dear beasts: they wonder why I want to cross over into their domain, but so it goes. They come sojourning down into our silly cities to inspect our oily machines and we come up here to impale ourselves on their branches. Also, I want to metamorphose myself, to shove my prodigious prodigy up Kate's sweet primeval cunt, to cross a few realms of my own. His leg throbbed with the weight of the covers, but he couldn't budge or his makeshift bedroll might leak.

Thunder. The rain started in earnest.

He stayed around his camp the next day because he felt that he couldn't make the walk back. Spreading his map on a stump, he studied shorter routes, but there were none, and soon he began thinking about not going out so soon, about possibly hiking up to Rainbow Glacier. It wasn't too far and he hadn't seen a glacier since he was eight or nine years old—when was it, Sarah, we stood on the edge of Grinnell Glacier?—and, besides, suicidal or not, it's the sort of thing I came for, he explained to himself, and he made estimates. Eight miles. Not too far, but another five thousand feet higher. I could make it up and back in three or four days—or weeks. He dared not look at his leg, but kept thinking about this additional torture.

With his repaired flyrod—cut down to one of the middle ferules—he took two more trout. The day passed pregnant with time, so that for a while it felt wasted, but then he began thinking, no, why must I always be doing something? Have my gears been fixed for production so that I can't drift? Settle down: run with the minutes, not against them; don't let the mind bully you out here.

That afternoon he caught sight of a mountain goat high on a ledge up on Cerulean Ridge and watched it through his binoculars until dark. For hours he didn't think about his injury. The goat, a white waif high up on that jut of rock, scrounged around doing nothing at all. That night he ate a large supper, his last big meal, he decided, until he came back from the glacier.

His leg felt swollen and tight the next morning, but he was beyond prudent considerations by that time and wanted to get on toward the glacier. But why? Because going up there will make me know something, he argued with himself; I'll stand on that deep blue ice, centuries old, older than the cities of the Orient, older than history and man's first gropings, and it will whisper to me. Stiffly, he walked around camp until his leg loosened up, then he left a note.

> Gone to Rainbow Glacier.
> Back in three days.

He dated it, signed his name, and started out again. By noon he had lost the trail—no man has walked up there for years, he knew—but didn't care. Following the line of Quartz Creek he began the steady climb, trusting his topographical map and the water flow; his plan was to reach Cerulean Lake above Quartz, then assault the mountain straight up the tree line to the glacier.

It was easier, at first, than he had thought. Following the white rush of the creek, crisscrossing, wading, climbing, marching through patches of sun-slanting forest, he reached Cerulean Lake early and started up. The day was bright, a few tatters of cloud overhead, and he felt particularly good; his leg throbbed, but no matter. Then the climb suddenly steepened and he found himself holding onto tree trunks, pulling himself up, or pausing at small chasms to hold his breath then jump across; the rocks refused him, slid from underfoot and scraped his hands. The glacier was just above him a few hundred yards, but the terrain became a cliff, a wall, and he became involved in a series of retreats and advances, searching this passage, that foothold. He spent hours with little progress and finally stopped. His body and the elements began their betrayal, then, as the night came on again. First, the wind came up and blew in a new cover of cold clouds from the north so that he could only sit there in his place between the rocks, burrowing into the soft dirt in that narrow crevice, wrapped in his bedroll and slicker. Howling, the wind became furious; nearby a branch—he was just at the timberline—broke and started a small avalanche. He was too cold to stir or eat or think. Inactive and stiffening, his body—the injury, especially—ached with the cold. He took the fetal position, curling his discomfort and breathing the insides of his bedroll: the musky odor of the old cloth, his own foul body and dried blood. When daylight came he shook off a light cover of snow that had blent him into the rocks.

Then upward again. He was thinking of nothing now, not Kate nor Sarah nor the butt ends of his life, not even his reasons for climbing. The wind whistled around him, punished his ears and nose, and his breath came in giant white puffs, labored. He had eaten only a piece of dried and flaky trout which he had cooked before starting on the trip, too, so that his stomach tightened and weakened him; the wind would blow out my matches if I tried a fire, he decided, and he thought of warm coffee and steaming biscuits.

Sheer rock now. He made his way sidelong, like a crab, over the face of his obstacle. Is that the cold mist of the glacier I smell, he asked himself, and am I near? Looking back, he could no longer see the lakes. A little farther on he spotted a field of snow, perhaps his goal, but he slipped down into another crevice, starving, to prepare his noon meal.

There were fossils in a wedge of rock in the crevice, remnants of a time—how long? half a billion years?—when all this had been the bed of a shallow sea. Millions of years later it had all been thrust upward in a gigantic fault, masses of rock, thousands of feet thick and miles long, to become the Rocky Mountains. Then the glaciers came: great moving masses of frozen river, cutting the rock into matterhorns and valleys. Your lectures, Sarah, yes, all of this. He nursed a small fire into life far back in a wedge of rock, heated dried milk then coffee in his single cup, then ate at least half of his dried beef. Delicious. Then a check on everything: his canteen was only half full, his food allotment was still sparse but okay, he could feel the wide lips of the gash on his leg through the wrappings. Up again and on the move.

The last climb capsized his senses; the wind whirled around him and threw him to the ground, once, like a dead branch. Tilting his body against it and driving upward, he reached the rim of the glacier before he realized it, then, finally knowing it, it simply didn't matter; the profundity he wanted escaped in his brittle pain; the leg throbbed from the fall, his head swam, the tears that formed on his eyelids from the gale around him turned to ice and became white scars. He went out onto the hard crust of snow—glacial gray-blue underneath—and stood there, gasping and small, and could only make for a stand of gnarled cedar off to his right. When he reached the trees, he slumped down saying, no, don't close your eyes or you'll fall asleep and die, no, don't.

Later that afternoon he followed the ridge down toward a nearby series of other smaller glaciers; he found the woods deep, the wind calmer, but his head raged and he felt addled and adream now in his exhaustion. Asleep again at dusk: his familiar dreamless, timeless slumber in that precious bedroll where he curled in thoughtless upon himself.

Other glaciers in view the next morning: ancient blisters on the slopes. He watched them in silence—the wind no longer an accompaniment—then moved on. That day he moved in a slow shuffle back toward his camp, pushing himself, his food gone, stopping twice to heat a cup of melted snow and drink instant coffee; he could feel his mouth grimly set.

A day passed while his senses ebbed back. Stripped, he lay on the bank of the lake sunning himself, his skin baking, and he was thinking, no, I didn't do this to find myself because I've always known exactly who I am, thank you, exactly: I am Baskin, myself alone since I was four years old and sassy, the solver of problems, loyal to duty, prideful, Sarah's driven offspring. And so did I do it to get away from Kate? Answer: yes. But more than that. I feel myself searching around in uncertain corners, thinking outside of the certainties of math and logic, for a change, pondering—what? Mysteries: the tiny regions where life gets better than its small sums.

With his finger he traced his face: a scab where he had cut himself in his fall, small skin peelings from sunburn, sunken eyes. A line of poetry bubbled up into his remembrance. *Downward to darkness on extended wings.* Does Kate read poetry? A vow: I should read some poetry sometime.

On the way back over the ridge to Polebridge the next morning his burden seemed curiously light, perhaps because he had eaten all the food, he decided, and he hurried along, kicking a stone out of his path, so that he could reach the store before it closed for the day and have himself a small gorge. He made excellent time at first until the lake lay far below, then he wearied again. Shit, my leg's killing me: this line began to amuse him so he started saying it aloud and laughing in his exhaustion.

A big stag, alert and haughty, greeted him on the path. Down, down, the pack pushed him downward. The glitter of the river finally came through the trees.

As he trudged into the ranger station the head ranger greeted him. "A lady was here looking for you," the ranger said, "and trying to form a search party this morning."

Baskin nodded, too tired to say much. "Where is she now?"

"Maybe over at the store."

"Well, I'll see her," Baskin said, and with a wave of his arm he went off across the Polebridge on the last half mile.

"From the looks of you," the ranger called after him, "she probably should've formed her search."

Baskin smiled, waved back once more, and kept walking.

At the store he dumped his pack into the Jeep, went inside and bought bread and lunch meat, and made himself sandwiches while sitting on the edge of the porch with his boots off. The sandwiches disappeared in a few bites, then as he drank a quart of milk he sat there contemplating his injury. The feel of being dirty: perfectly fine. His weariness inebriated him and made him want to giggle.

Kate drove up in the old station wagon just as he began to unwrap his makeshift bandage. The car stopped in an impressive cloud of dust and she got out and sauntered toward him: same tight jeans, same deadly walk, so that he remembered quickly why he had to get out of the house. Then, as she came near her face began to alter.

"Baskin?" she asked, as if he weren't.

"Hi," he managed, and he kept unwrapping his leg as she dropped down beside him on her lovely haunches. She peered into his face with curiosity and surprise, and, oh, keep looking at me like that, he wanted to tell her, and never take your eyes off, and kiss me hello.

Then the bandage came off and there it was in all its terrible beauty.

"Oh, Baskin," she whispered, and for a moment her lower lip quivered, as if she were about to cry—which, of course, Kate would never do—and her face became so beautiful, so rare, the way no one had ever looked at him before, not even Sarah, and he was out on the cold blue glacier again, not at all cold, standing out there with his arms outstretched and yodeling, calling to the mountains, singing and feeling profound, and it was all he could do to return her gaze. He wanted to say that there was this bear, this huge bear.

❧ IX ❧

The doctor visited, Baskin was stitched and patched, the summer bloomed, Kate was there and the sparring began.

"What made you think you could take on the great outdoors like that anyway?"

"It's my outdoors. I grew up here."

"You grew up standing at a blackboard in a little apartment in a dirty city."

"I was raised outdoors. Right here."

"The most grass you ever saw in one place was at Comiskey Park."

"Oh, that just isn't so. I had eight long years here with Sarah."

"You were too young to remember that, though—"

"How many times do I have to tell you? I don't *forget* things!"

"Total recall, eh?"

"Right!"

"I'm pouring your coffee now. Think you can make it over here to the window seat by yourself?"

"Ask me about the summer when I was five years old! Ask me what I did on the first Monday of June that year, go ahead."

"You'll make something up."

"I'll tell you exactly what—"

"Poor dear. So abnormally gifted. It must have been awful missing the simple life. Sandlot baseball. High school assembly programs. All that."

"What's an assembly program?"

"Ah, you see. Well, in public schools all of us endured these wonderful events every week. Let's see, there was the man who came to our school to whistle bird calls. Another time we had the man who played the electric accordion and another time—hmm, it might have been the same fellow—we had the juggler who kept six plates in the air while lecturing us on good health habits. Want your coffee or not?"

"That was public education?"

"Sure, see what you missed?"

"Just half a spoon of sugar, please."

No doubt of it: Kate was warm toward him now and when they talked she seemed to casually reveal herself to him as she did that first night down on the road in the snowstorm, but she was also contentious, argumentative, and usually difficult, too. Sarah's old style, he caught himself feeling: the same banter and minor bickering.

Yet, all different. Her hair seemed to catch the sun wherever she walked and she was always turning, pressing the thrust of her breasts against her shirt, drawing her waist thin like a bow, arching toward him, so that the new summer heat fell on him and rose out of him all at once.

He limped for days and had a slight fever off and on. But he soon sensed the advantage of his wound, how it insured her attention if not her sympathy and how she came around to ask him about himself. The days of grief and the business of Sarah's passing were clearly gone, he knew, and Kate had been left alone—oh, good move—while he lingered out there in the wilderness so that she was suddenly social now, though fussy, and needing him. At times, she became abruptly personal.

"What about girls? Any girls in your life in New Orleans?"

"Sarah and I had the same rule: we never talked much about ourselves. Pick a subject, any subject. I'll show you myself, but I won't tell you about myself. Is that fair?"

"Oh, you're bashful—"

"It's a rule of mine."

"Well, it wasn't Sarah's rule, believe me. She talked about herself."

"She made rules so she could break them. I'm a keeper of rules."

"You're self-possessed—too much so."

"See, you're making up your mind about me. I don't have to talk about myself at all. What would I say? Something self-congratulatory? I think I'm wonderful."

"You're like all men."

"Shit."

"You're all alike."

Most of the time in one curious way or another she made him angry. A slight condescension, a small assault here or there. She seemed to thrust him away, then demand that he open himself up; and he recalled, *either you beat the men or get beaten by them,* and watched her new daily routine as she got into the habit of stalking off to the new bunkhouse every morning to practice her writing. What was she *writing?* Did she have any talent? As much as Sarah's, at least? Did she have a single weapon so that she could defend herself against all the male adversaries she imagined for herself downworld? In the early afternoons she'd come back to the lodge, prepare a small lunch, ask after his health, observe a few niceties, then pick at him a little. A gentle probe, then bitchiness.

There must be rituals here I just don't understand, he decided. Perhaps there's some strange ordeal by the blood's fire I must go through, something I must suffer in order to find the key. Or is there a key? Is there a thing women want?

He remembered himself as one who could stare down the coldest of full professors. A drooling vice-president had courted his favor—this was just after he left Chicago —wanting him to work with a company's cretin engineers and he had said, ah, no thanks, and when at lunch he had spilled gravy on his tie the vice-president had agreeably spilled a little himself because he was so awed. Scientists, intellectuals, the very rich: none of these bothered him. But he felt a slight tremor—a deep nausea of terror—with Kate. And why? Surly waiters, bankers, men like Dierker, what of them? But women: damn, it was something else again.

One day he noticed that she had put the binoculars on the window seat. From the bay window he could see across the meadow where the bunkhouse was in plain view at the river's bend. Picking them up, he scanned the area. River rocks, the white foam of the water as it curved around the chute at the far point, each single blade of deep green grass came into sight, but no Kate. Doesn't she want me to spy on her? He began to think of ways to lure her away from the place so that he could inspect the bunkhouse.

The opportunity came soon and naturally enough; she had to make another trip down to Polebridge for groceries and he made excuses to stay at the ranch. As soon as the last dust had settled behind her on the road, he made a dash down the meadow. Everything was unlocked, so he toured through it hurriedly; he inspected the sun porch, the bunk rooms, the card room with the fireplace, the bath and locker room, but found nothing. No stack of manuscript, no worried wastebaskets, not even a pencil. Does she bury her scribblings, he wondered, so that no mere man may find them? There was no real sign of her in the place, in fact: no hairpins, clothes, stray lipsticks. Mystery Woman Meets Boy Wonder. Okay, here's a pad on the sundeck where she stretches out in the sun, but so what? Did she leave the binoculars so I could see her here? No, from the bay window I couldn't see this side of the porch.

Back at the lodge, his fantasies galloped over him.

Then Max Neuborn called. He and his wife and his brother-in-law were planning to go up to the border and float the river for some fishing, and, yes, Baskin said, put in here, and come for dinner, sure, you'll be tired after your day on the water. A social evening was arranged. It's well enough, he told himself. I'll get my mind off the situation here. So when Kate came back they at least had that to plan, yet she didn't seem too pleased. "I don't have the right food and can't get it at Polebridge," she complained. "I'll have to drive back down to West Glacier."

"Oh, why do that? Feed them trout and potatoes."

"You don't know anything about how much trouble it is keeping this place going, do you?" she snapped like an angry housewife.

"What's that supposed to mean?"

"You just live inside your head. That's what I mean. You never fret over practical matters: who makes the beds, how the food gets on the table, whether the pine needles get swept or not."

"I've taken care of myself for a long time perfectly well," he told her.

"And while we're on the subject," she went on, "we ought to work out some fair way of paying for things. It's all so damned haphazard. You write a check sometimes, then I write a check, but, god, I lose track. Let's set up a proper budget."

"Anything you say."

"We at least ought to spend Sarah's money in equal shares."

"Fine, make a budget."

"And now I'll have to drive all the way back down for better groceries. To feed the Neuborns. I'm not even sure I like them."

"Want me to go to West Glacier?"

"You wouldn't know what to buy. You'd come home with frozen minute steaks."

"Shall I write you a check for the groceries, then?"

"That's *not* what I was talking about. In general, I meant. We have to work out something fair about the money in general."

"Oh."

When Kate left again, Baskin went back and smiled at himself in the bathroom mirror and gave himself a shrug. Then he stood there admiring his sunburnt face. Aren't I getting thinner, too? I look older, stronger. The trek up to the glacier did something for me. I'm a man. Boyhood gone. So why do I let Kate stall me? Look here, take off those silly blue jeans and come here. C'mere, open up, there, kiss me or I'll slap the sneer off your mouth.

Days passed in such reverie. Back in his loft he retreated into sleep once again. Kate fussed with dinner preparations and worried that the Neuborns wouldn't eat a congealed salad.

The dinner that evening turned out badly anyway because the Neuborns kept trying to ease a mild criticism of Sarah into the conversation—she was a bit wild and silly, wasn't she? ha ha, always breaking her back trying to be slightly different, that sort of thing—and neither Baskin nor Kate much appreciated it. Also, the brother-in-law, some divorced slob from lower California, kept leering at Kate. Called her baby. And, finally, the Neuborns and the brother-in-law wanted to parade their social consciousness and they went on about the war, the never-ending war, emerging African nations, the poor in the cities, pollution, the ecological necessities, and Baskin felt himself drifting away from them every minute.

Neuborn: "Were you ever in Mensa, Baskin?"

Baskin: "No."

Neuborn: "Jan's brother here is a member of Mensa, aren't you, Jack?"

Jack: "That's right. I thought you'd be a member, too, kid."

Baskin: A slow closing and opening of the eyelids, dismissing the conversation.

Then Neuborn got back to Sarah, mentioning her nudism in a somewhat ambiguous and embarrassed way and saying, "You know your mother was a little off, Baskin." And he brought up the subject of the letter—which he called an eccentric document—and he talked about how all the people in the Northfork didn't ever know what to make of her, how she wouldn't attend their square dances at the Community Hall and how she had so many ranch hands, more than she needed. The innuendoes got thick and it was all Baskin could do to sit there.

So they talked politics again, the brother-in-law putting in a good word for "liberal responsibility" until Baskin couldn't take any more and stood up and rested his hand on the shortwave radio and said simply, "Some of us create the society by creating ourselves, baby."

"Now what do you mean by that?" Neuborn put in. "Define your terms."

"He means that some people have enough personal value so that as they work out their own private system of things they do the society the greatest service," Kate said. "Or I'll put it plainer: Baskin needs to be left alone for his own work."

"In fact, I think I'll go to bed," Baskin said.

"You do that," Kate said. "I'll stay here and explain things for them."

Baskin felt a surge of unspeakable giddiness. Kate defending me. The Neuborns and the brother-in-law were making sudden rebuttals, saying that wasn't what they had meant at all.

"But let me say one thing about my mother before I go," Baskin added. "Mama's eccentricity was her sanity. You're the goddamned crazy ones, after all, in your neat jobs, your neat lives." He delivered all this with only mild irritation.

Neuborn was on his feet. "Look here, I didn't mean to start anything."

Then it was continuing, voices louder, but Baskin was making his way up to the loft. He could hear Kate quieting them and not long afterward he heard them at the door, saying their goodnights, and moments later listened as their car pulled away.

All quiet. He lay there with his head back on his pillow for a long while, until he heard Kate's footsteps below the loft. She seemed to come to the stairway, pause, and wait for him; for a moment he felt his body tighten and he started to rise and go down, but she walked away.

The next morning after she had gone down to the

bunkhouse he found the binoculars again on the window seat.

He fixed them on the bunkhouse. Nothing. Then he turned them up toward Mt. Kintla and searched the rocks for a ram or an eagle's nest.

Kate: clusters, clusters everywhere about her now, but he didn't know her at all.

He could recite the information of her life: growing up in West Dallas, the alcoholic father, the marriage to get away from it all, the young husband who dreamt of owning a ranch in Oklahoma, working her way through college as a secretary while she encountered a few professors. Afterward she went to Chicago, counting on her looks, she said, to keep her near men who had a little more intelligence and money until she found one, Ray McCluskey, who of course didn't do at all. "All this time I was angling and conning," she said. "But I was in the men's world—close to something—and not whining outside it like a mistress or housewife on an allowance." The husband's first girl friends she even ignored. Every day she stood at the wire service at that suburban newspaper and felt "on top of something, with it" and knew if she backed off without a proper apprenticeship there might be no second chances. When she finally left the man— who happened to own the paper—she announced she wanted no alimony, nothing really material, just a recommendation, a letter full of hyperbole, please, Ray, so that another editor someplace would hire her. "Say I'm the most exciting writer you've ever had on the staff," she asked of him. "Say I'm diligent and brilliant and that I'll win the Pulitzer Prize. I mean it, Ray, do it. Save yourself some alimony and do me that huge favor." And it was done. She went to Mexico with the letter written, going off for that first precious solitude while she gathered herself together. She drove around from town to town in Ray's Porsche (which she promised to return and did) and felt lonely and wistful, like a young girl, at times, and other days like a hardened bitch, all leathery and weather-worn, and time became a corrosive force then a mender of all it had inflicted. One night in Tampico, a really bad town with *las playas* littered with trash and human dung and rotted fish entrails, she said, she allowed a man to pick her up. A shabby fat Mexican baker who had come out on the jetty for a breath of foul evening air after his day's work. They went to his shack down the beach— Baskin hated remembering this part—and she wouldn't lie down on his dirty bed, but let him do it to her as she sat back on the edge of his oilclothed table and smelled his heavy odor of flour and sweat and thought of nothing, nothing at all, just let him burrow into her. Then she went back to Chicago, returned the car, said thanks very much, and looked for jobs. Editors, advertising men, assistants to publishers: everyone wanted to put her on the edge of a desk, on the couch in the inner office, on a hotel mattress down the street, but few would give her more than occasional assignments. For a while she wrote copy for a shoe company, nothing usable. Then Sarah: an idle phone call in answer to an ad and a friend at last. They sat there while Baskin worked physics problems—you hummed, she reminded him, while the chalk dust flew—

and talked over Dierker and Ray McCluskey and the dreary divisions of the world, talked about menstrual cramps and money, about books that had moved them. "It was as though we were caught in a cosmic blast, in the big bang, and as though we were moving away from everything and everything was moving away from us at tremendous speed. I felt myself zooming away from the world and Sarah felt you zooming away from her—even then—so we clung to talk, lots of talk, and our voices, oh, Baskin, were *so* reassuring."

All this had come to Baskin in fragments of talk, idle exposures, but he had stored it up—and not even because he believed Kate to be the sum of all this. She was more: all this just the pool in which she was mirrored, he knew, because he was like that too.

"By the time your mother and I became friends," she admitted once, "I felt like a raging feminist. Like a runaway slave talking to another runaway slave in a hiding place. The question was how to live, how to go back into a world that conspired against you." Sarah had it worked out. She had her corny westerns to write, her marketable product. But it must have been more difficult for Kate, Baskin imagined, and still difficult for her now.

So Kate and Sarah were in New York together. They rented a studio apartment together in the East Sixties, something more than Kate could have dreamed to live in, and hired a maid and rented a car when they wanted one so that Sarah could glide around like a friendly spy and keep track of her son and so that they could occasionally get out together, up to the Cloisters, for instance, or out to Long Island on weekends. They went to museums, plays, everything that opened at Lincoln Center. Dierker took them both to dinner once or twice—the talk, Kate said, was all the boy genius—though Sarah refused to see

him as much as Dierker asked and never, to Kate's knowledge, alone. And they worked on a book, *Aspen Trail,*
with Kate acting as secretary-idea girl. A lousy book, low
on shoot-outs, void of logical transitions. The talk continued, too, her post-graduate course in reality, Kate said.
What Baskin wanted to know, though, was something
deeper: how Sarah regarded her inmost self by this time
and how she regarded him and what Kate felt. But he
and Kate were yet to have such discussions. He could
only know how they lived, some of the things they did;
he hadn't asked Kate all he wanted to ask, so that in all
the data which had accumulated the final insights just
weren't there.

Besides, he hated himself for thinking on and on about
all this. He cut a hundred cords of wood—or so it seemed
—pondering these tidbits of biography and gossip. My
head has been full of molecular theory, equations, measurements, formulas, units of light and now I've tumbled
backward into adolescent musings. Or is that really re-
gression in my case? Am I getting the blocks of a life finally, the stuff to build an emotional existence? Is that Sarah's real legacy?

Each time he worried about his preoccupation with all
this, however, his body made it seem inevitable. He woke
up mornings with a gigantic erection, his first thoughts a
continuing dream of Kate. After his shower he'd stand at
the mirror observing his slimmer self: hardened arms, a
new tan, the wide scar which served as an emblem of a
new identity. There you are, he'd say, addressing his
lovely lower part. Hammer of Thor, you are attached to a
meek and mind-boggled waif. Great Wooer of the World,
you hang from an abstract soul. Once more today, dearest
dork, Baskin's mind will hold court and study all the conditions of the case and you will wait in his pants like the

star witness not yet called to testify. Standing at the mirror with a certain pride in his nakedness, he'd say it outright: I'm thinking of you today again, my Fate, my Kate, regarding you like a dedicated and thorough scholar, but how can I possibly know your mysteries until I've mystically fucked your mystic body?

How to do it.

The great and ghastly question.

He took long walks on the property, managed a flyrod across the river rocks, stood very still in the midday glare while a mosquito autographed his wrist.

A letter from Dierker came:

Surprise. I'm coming back, as I promised. Your money in hand, Baskin, and a little something by way of interest on it, just a small present. If you can pick me up at the Sandersons' ranch about noon on the 28th, that'll be grand. Shouldn't have any trouble landing there in this good weather. How's the fishing? How about a hello kiss, old Kate?

As always, D.

Kate read it after Baskin and surprised him with a comment. "You loaned him some money?" she asked.

"That's right."

"It's an old trick of his. One he played on Sarah."

"What do you mean?"

"He didn't need the money at all," Kate said. "He just wanted to get into your debt. It's a psychological thing he worked on you."

That sent him off alone—he went to the library to peruse Sarah's books—to think things out again. Do people play those kinds of games? Is it all that tough making contact? Answer: yes. And, again, Kate knows so much more the ways of things than I do. I'll never get through the summer; everything out here is natural except me and the stars are up there mocking my hang-ups and the mountains diminish me and Kate must think I'm ridiculous.

That afternoon he started working out a few equations at Sarah's desk and when Kate asked him what he was doing he said, "Oh, getting a little work done. I can't just sit around here all the time." Kate glanced over his shoulder at the splash of his handwriting, the impenetrable jumble of numbers, and he felt a small advantage again. But feeling advantages still wasn't what he wanted.

❧ XI ❧

The distance Baskin now felt from the world, he realized, was one he had arranged himself, and it had started, deliberately, back with Sarah at certain dark points along their life together. It was a widening spiral away from each other to be sure, but it hadn't started before Chicago; here at the ranch before he had been in a naked neutral gear, no sweat. It was, looking back, an almost utopian time, nearly too perfect, and perhaps the competitive drag of the university later simply proved too much of a contrast. Oh, there were a few rough moments; Sarah would occasionally drive him too hard. Once, far back— he must have been almost five because he was mastering multiplication—she was urging him on. It was the time she had devised some shortcuts for him and he wanted to go down and play at the river. "You don't have to multiply by each separate number in a series," she was explaining to him. "Suppose, say, Baskin, you want to multiply by the number five thousand two hundred and fifty."

"Multiplying by five thousand is easy," he said, sighing. "I know. Just multiply by five and add the zeroes."

"That's right. But now you can multiply by two

hundred and fifty, too, dear, by just quartering the number being multiplied. See?"

"I want to build a rock house just now."

"Just a minute longer on this, please."

"If we wait, the sun'll go down and I'll get chilly. I want to now."

"See how I'm doing it here?"

"You know the weather report was for a new cold mass late this afternoon. Why not let us play n-now?"

"Do this first."

"I just don't want to."

"I'll give you an ice cream."

"Give me an hour at the river—now."

"You have your reading this evening. I want some progress today on this quick multiplication system."

"Progress," he sighed. "I'm going out."

"Then no ice cream."

"I'd rather play. And build a rock house."

"Then build it yourself. I'm staying in."

"Why? To work the problems?"

"I suppose. You go ahead and build a rock house by yourself."

"Oh, all right. I'll do the silly problems. What now? Divide the n-number by a quarter and what?"

Her tactics consisted of a series of bribes, brags, urgings, pleas, threats and noble speeches on the exalted life of the intellect. She rewarded him with too many foods and desserts which made him fat. She told him that he was the brightest child in the history of great prodigies, and he beamed. One autumn—in his sixth year—he became religious for five whole weeks. This was soon after Sarah's crash course on the religions of Western man.

"I feel like praying, Mama," he told her at supper one evening.

"What?"

"Praying. Like the boy on the cover of *Saturday Evening Post*."

"Oh, all right, go ahead, Baskin. Put your hands together in the proper way."

He prayed for an indian summer, but on October 15 they received ten inches of snow and winter set in with a fury. He prayed for a new bicycle, but Sarah gave him a sled. He prayed for another trip to the Bahamas, but Sarah's order for new textbooks arrived. By Thanksgiving Day he was a heathen again.

Sarah kept igniting him, and looking back, now, he could remember the times he actually caught fire, how he went spinning off into projects with his childish adrenalin pumping; at the piano he broke into furious compositions, banging out chords and descants, leaning forward to get it down on composition paper like a mad young Mozart, begging Sarah, then, to play it for him. His little nocturnes and sonatas filled the rafters. Or he would get into a sudden frenzy over an experiment. Once, as a joke on Sarah, he went around gathering all his chemical compounds and mixing vigorously and peeking into his microscope and dashing off secret formulas in his notebook until she asked him what he was doing. He wouldn't tell her and the secret grew. Then, impishly, he swiped three of her Alka Seltzers and crushed them into a powder which he dyed blue with a food coloring. "Come see! Come see!" he yelled at her and she ran from the kitchen —she was wearing only an apron—and at the moment of her arrival he poured the powder into a glass of red water and a bright purple fizz erupted. Sarah's eyes widened. "Ha! I've done it!" he cried and he laughed a long Mad Scientist cackle until Sarah shivered with terror, then, as the purple Seltzer sputtered and popped he held it aloft, cackled again, and drank it off. "Baskin!" she screamed, and knocked the glass out of his hand and he rolled in laughter, hysterical. Or he wrote his famous short story, "The Man on the Mountain," which he read aloud to her one cold winter night by the fireside. In the story the old hermit's face was lashed by snow as he went in search of his faithful dog, Shep, and in the end the old man was discovered dead and frozen and Shep howled at the cold moon and Baskin wrote that "Life is brutal," which he learned, of course, from Jack London, but Sarah dutifully wept and put her arms around him and gave him an extra pudding.

In those days she drove him, yes, but usually such projects kept him toiling on his own. And he could see, later, that he had enjoyed the advantage of the only valid sort of education, deep and earnest private instruction which is valid because of its emotional texture, its excitement and tender care. That was it, put simply: Sarah cared and he cared and out of those seasons came the necessary passion.

Then Chicago.

Long before Lothridge and the more sophisticated professors there had been a squadron of young teachers who had worked with him, eager scholars who wanted to fathom the nature of his prodigy, lead him on to greater achievements, and, of course, play a little one-up-manship with him. They seemed helpful enough and Baskin enjoyed all the attention—he knew he was being observed frequently through the one-way mirror by another battery of psychologists—and when they finally got around to their slight condescensions he held his own with them. But Sarah didn't like them. At first she had to explain that they were covering a lot of the old ground in math which Baskin had already mastered, but they had to see for themselves. Then she made some pedagogical suggestions: how they could coax him along with candy bars, how they had to let him rest from mid-afternoon on, and how they had to give him variety—many artistic and scientific enterprises, difficult but mixed. The young profs took her advice at first (Baskin soon weighed one hundred pounds and was of about the same texture and shape as a marshmallow because of all the candy they supplied him), yet there she stood, dumpy and chatty and emotional, so that soon they wanted Baskin to themselves. Naturally he learned to play everyone against everyone else. From Sarah he demanded and received his first dress suits—because he wanted to look professorial. From the young profs he demanded and got an office with his name on the door. It was a playful illusion, that office, but curiously important; in essence, the young prodigy-in-residence was a faculty member at nine years of age.

"Is Mr. Baskin in today?" they would inquire, knocking lightly and grinning.

"Come on in, guys."

"How about a little quiz this morning, Mr. Baskin? Would you like to work a few brainbusters for us today?"

"Fine, but listen, would one of you mind going down and sharpening my pencils for me before I s-start?"

"Sure, buddy. Anything else?"

"Well, it's a bit stuffy in the building this morning. How about a Coke?"

The liberal education Sarah had offered was mostly finished as the young professors urged him to concentrate on his math skills and his chemistry talents. Time, time, he could say to himself now; it took me in its grip, saying, Solve Problems, Get Something Done, Learn Ambition. The university offered among other things its peculiar vanity.

In the late afternoons and nights he still belonged to Sarah, though, and they went to sit behind third base, watching Minnie Minoso spear line drives, pound his glove, spit, stab hot grounders, fire his rifle shots to first base. The sky above Comiskey Park was dark sapphire. The arc lights glamorized the world. With baseball and other small maneuvers Sarah sought to keep her son for —for what? She never said it outright, but surely, he knew, she coveted his life for something less sterile and less certain than the mathematical cubicles which the young profs were pressing on him. Something romantic. Hence, baseball. Hence, more music—and urgent lectures while he listened—and more movies and more food and more desperation hugs. "Hear that now. Listen hard, Baskin," she'd hiss at him during the Beethoven, but even with his eyes closed he could feel her eyes on him, weighing his responses, and he could smell the faint aroma of her perspiration there in the hush of the theater and the first murmurs of his disgust gathered. "Let me alone if you want me to listen," he'd hiss back at her, and the next day, somehow, he would deepen his allegiance to the labs, his university projects and the young profs. A nag, that's what she is. Such a simple way of seeing her, but he could remember saying it over and over like a liturgy.

The years went on, all the doting psychologists parted, and Baskin, by his twelfth year, was a campus fixture. Except for Sarah, life there proceeded filled with tranquil habits; he took his lunch with two young grad students, Weihmeyer and Burgess, at the Commons and they walked around on the lawns afterward when the weather permitted viewing the coeds. Burgess, who wanted to do medical research, would bad mouth the girls, saying things under his breath like, "Up yours sideways, honey-pot," and other such profound assertions and Baskin and Weihmeyer would turn their heads in embarrassment, laugh, and help Burgess get ready for the next girl strolling innocently along the promenade. After his afternoon lab work or a library session Baskin would meet Sarah for dinner. She had a new novel out that year and money had flowed in so that they dined out frequently; she had resorted to the bright approach by this time and always smilingly asked him what he had done with his day and made conversation, but their trouble had definitely set in. By this time, also, the young profs had given him over to some of the more renowned professors—Lothridge, for example—and he was at least at the start of his first original research in chemistry. Lothridge and Jurgens, his two favorite old gentlemen, helped him to devise his first project: a series of experiments by which he could possibly gauge more accurately the radioactivity of some meteorite fragments which the university owned. Days, weeks, months went along at this and Sarah gave up trying to entertain him in the evenings because he was usually so irritable. She suggested that he go to the campus psychiatric clinic once, "Just for, you know, a little weekly therapy so you won't get mentally exhausted in your work." But he said no.

In the winter of his twelfth year he took the flu. He stayed at the campus infirmary, tried to get going too soon, suffered a relapse, and had to spend a week at home in the apartment with Sarah. She was awfully pushy, trying to get him to read Shakespeare some more and he thought, oh, god, here we go again; I'm trying to determine the age of the stars and she wants me to experience the balcony scene. Then one afternoon she went out to the drugstore and his hands found himself under the covers and suddenly, stretching every muscle, shaking his sickness off, a new sensation began to rise in him and he spiraled away, his thoughts raging hot, and he saw a vision of the coed assistant in Lothridge's lab over at the Institute; he threw the covers off. There, across the white paunch of his belly, the great beauty rose up in all its blue-veined splendor and he took it in hand, inventing the poor lab assistant's sprawling body in his mind's eye, and he stroked himself only once, twice, three times and out it gushed all white and sticky and, ah, damn, oh Burgess and Mama and oh jesus Dr. Lothridge I'm a man. It ran down into his softhair and when he jumped up, giddy, it gushed again, a drop spotting Sarah's precious oriental throw rug, and ran down his leg. Jubilantly, he hobbled to the bathroom. Skipped back to wipe the spot. Dried himself tenderly. Danced to the window to see if Sarah was coming back down the street. Dove back into bed, covered up, grabbed it again. I Dedicate My Dork to Science. I Will Discover the Truth: how many geysers possible in one hour, one day, one lifetime; how many beats to the geyser; geysers and nuclear energy. He dreamt of all the girls he had ever seen, all that had stirred him and some who hadn't, all of them giving him siren calls now across the oasis of the bed, and rolling his eyes gave himself a super-doublestroke and ejaculated into his palm just as Sarah ejaculated through the door, laden with packages and shopping bags, so that they suddenly stared at each other in a panting hello. He sank beneath the covers where his heart drove like a wild piston and when she made her way through the room and into the kitchen with her load he dashed for the bathroom again.

"How're you feeling?" she asked a few minutes later.

Warm and different, his glowing cheeks replied.

So with puberty, as usual, the mother-son distance grew and out of this new change came Sarah's deepest frustration. She brought forth stacks of modern novels—

Bellow, Böll, Sillitoe, Durrell, Mishima—trying an appeal to his literary humanity, and also a pile of new records, everything from Segovia to The Dave Clark Five, but work and sex—mostly work, alas—were driving him along. Pimples sprouted. His stutter became more severe.

In his thirteenth year, then, when his thoughts were dizzied with sex and when Sarah was fussing at him and his confident professors seemed excited to find his physical and mental limits, the pressures built and he started his retreat. Turned in and down on myself, he recalled now; down, down into the tiny quiet place in the mind where dreams are stored. The sexual urge, for instance, was pathetic; he was still a boy-child physically, all plump and white like some species of featherless bird, so that no girl would even consider him. Yet he burned. A small collection of pornography accumulated among the stacks of *Scientific American* in his closed office and between the thighs of those anonymous sweetmeats his private theater flourished. But, also, his experiments with the meteorites had come to nothing and he felt—though he couldn't have articulated it then—the same kind of anguish that might be felt by a junior instructor who had to impress the deans and regents in order to keep his position. In the late afternoons, overworked, he walked home beneath the bare limbs of the winter trees, sighing, his briefcase almost dragging the ground. He set up his kitchen blackboard at this time and kept up his formula-tossing at night after supper. After Sarah had forced him out to a movie or the Ice Capades or a ballet or a hockey match he went back to the kitchen for a late snack and more chalking. And there she was, always, reading his ingrown life; she nagged him, he knew now, as one might poke around embers with a stick. She wanted his happy childhood to burst into flame again.

His birthday party at the Faculty Club. She spent a week organizing it. The little waitress with the missing blouse button.

When he was fourteen Lothridge asked if he didn't want to set up his own degree program. "Let's say you're in the first year of your doctoral program now, Baskin, just to be academic for a moment. Now in lots of ways, of course, you're far beyond that point, but there are some things you should consider yet, too—some areas in which you could be considered behind. And I've been thinking. Perhaps, you know, your mother's right. You might want to take some studies elsewhere, too. In your music, say, or in the liberal arts."

"N-no, I'll stick with all this," Baskin said smiling. "I'm at home in the labs."

"Then we'll push on toward a degree, I think, Baskin. You ought to get out into some work eventually and away from here." It was one of those moments when Lothridge broke over into his stern self, acting fatherly, yet Baskin knew he was right. The last months had come. Good-bye Commons. Good-bye Gothic ivy. Good-bye Burgess, dear professor, omnipotent Mama.

Sensing the coming of the end, Sarah tried everything.

"Let's whip over to Europe this spring," she suggested. "Maybe spend the whole summer."

"I can't."

"Get a small villa. Someplace where they wear bikinis or less. You need to be around girls, right?"

"I need to w-work this spring. You know it."

Life, all this time, accelerated in strange ways. Within a period of months he seemed to pass from his fierce early puberty into a calm of greater control. All the adolescent and early periods took brief forms: a talkative, gossipy stage which he filled with stories about his professors and acquaintances; a surly stage during which he talked to no one and felt sad about the war in Asia; sophomore cynicism—about two bitter weeks of it; an artistic period during which he composed two short pieces of music for piano and flute, a wistful short story, and an unmailed letter to Dierker along the lines of Kafka's famous letter to his father; and finally a time when he became earnest about his career and had long talks with Weihmeyer about which Eastern schools might be more prestigious. All these phases were moments. They lasted weeks, sometimes days. His social life, like his mind, leapt through time and speedy evolution.

"I'm nothing if not quick," he remarked to Burgess one afternoon as they sucked up malted milks at the Commons.

"You're quick, but you're nothing, too," said Burgess, who was in his own cynical period and meant it in the cosmic sense.

At fourteen Baskin had handled sex in the simplest way by repressing it, but Sarah had somehow got stuffed away with it down in the dark recesses of his nether-mind. She was a bother he simply couldn't think about because she hurt. Nothing personal, he wanted to tell her. I'm just beyond mothers and motherly flutterings forever. Yet it was personal. Her stockings bagged, she sounded like one of those older frustrated intellectuals who had never had a hearing and demanded one, and she could be casual about nothing. As he became cooler, then, her style became a holocaust and he could say to himself, ah hell, I know I'm driving you to act this way, yet what shall I do?

Cluster: a balmy day in June, 1965. Sarah bouncing around naked in the apartment with a glass of iced tea reading one of my textbooks.

"Put on some goddamned clothes! You think I want to

look at your short hair? What if someone came over?"

"Who'd come over? Burgess? It'd do him good."

"Shit, Mama, get dressed. I got no earthly oedipal interest in seeing any of that again."

"Who said you have to? The body is a natural phenomenon. A lovely tree with lovely limbs, even when they're poochy like mine. Besides, damn, aren't you hot? Let's go out to the park or to a movie."

Cluster: at lunch with Lothridge in the Commons. Sarah materializes with a stack of her novels under her arm, smiling at us and breaking into our conversation and taking a seat with her creations dribbling onto the floor.

"Yours, Sarah?"

"That's right, professor. Brought them for you. For your leisure hours at home."

"Thank you very much."

"Mama, please. Jesus Christ."

Cluster: Sarah standing with her back against the door having just come back from a date with some man. Her eyes are shut. Tears on her cheek. She has just left his automobile out on the street and there she stands with some of her own inner life glistening on her face; we have our own secret selves, sure, Mama as well as I, but we're distant satellites now, turning in a widening orbit. I peer out from my stance at the kitchen blackboard and there she is, slumping against the door; one of the brain's permanent records.

It was later, toward the last months of the Chicago degree, that Sarah dated so much. Where she found the men Baskin didn't know, but she learned his lab schedule, he knew, and he could tell sometimes that the Kimbark Avenue apartment had been mussed with her middle-aged pursuits and skirmishes. Then she began another

123

book, something about wildcatting for oil so that she had to advertise for research help, and Kate appeared on the scene. Kate, ah yes: she was reading a French woman— probably Simone de Beauvoir—and taking lessons in Tae Kwon Do and karate. (It all fits together now, Baskin thought, remembering the early forms of her feminist philosophy.) And with Kate's arrival, or soon afterward, Sarah stopped seeing her parade of men and the two of them talked, yes, all day and all night, and went down to The Loop to shop and linger and talk some more. Thinking back, Kate seemed much the same—of an indefinite age, certainly not girlish although younger by far than Sarah. By this time, too—ah, yes, an index to my control and dear repression—Kate didn't even seem particularly sexy. She was Mama's friend, the one who required a pot of coffee to get started in the mornings, nothing more. She wore slacks and heavy sweaters—no bra, probably— and wore her hair pulled tightly back and falling in a single heavy ponytail. Once she came back and propped herself in the doorway while I tossed up some equations and her face was etched with wonder; childishly, he thought, I didn't even notice her and just went on working aware that she sort of vaguely admired me.

In the last weeks, then, thoughts of the immediate future rattled around in his forebrain. In the midst of his prelims the dean of the graduate school called Lothridge into conference and discussed whether or not Baskin might fit into a New York job. Yes, naturally. Old Dr. Ludmiller came up with a job for him, too. The dean of another school who had read an article on Baskin also came to town to win his favor. Business lunches flowered everywhere. Baskin favored New York because it allowed him freedom to work on his own with a group of physicists, chemists and radiation experts and also because he'd live in Greenwich Village; occasionally, amidst all the talk of career and position, he managed to dream of hip girls who would visit his walk-up flat. They would play sordid music and dance naked in the dark; exhausted with sex they'd stroll MacDougal Street, munch hot dogs, share a few dreams.

"It's New York, then," Lothridge finally said. "And such an honor for you! Sarah's going to be so damned proud."

"I'm not telling her about the job," Baskin warned. "This is it between us. I've got to get away from her."

Lothridge never replied, never looked up.

⇝ XII ⇜

Dierker's pilot flew him into a neighboring rancher's summer landing strip where Kate and Baskin met him. They embraced, shook hands, unloaded his baggage and a heavy crate, then went back to the ranch for some lunch and afternoon riding. It was the sort of greeting Dierker liked: a display of affection, food and recreation.

By evening, though, Baskin was restless and put off by the fact that Dierker seemed to talk mostly to Kate. It's Kate he's visiting all right, Baskin assured himself. He doesn't fly across the country for a breath of mountain air, oh no, and now there's a free track to Kate with Mama gone. All through supper, too: Dierker told Kate stories about mutual acquaintances in New York, discussed his business, and finally brought out the crate which they had unloaded that noon, the gift for Baskin, presumably, which as it turned out was to be opened by Kate. It's for both of you, really, he told them, and Kate dug down and there they were: Sarah's novels, all bound in brown leather with gold lettering.

"Oh, Dierker," Kate said, and she seemed genuinely touched so that Baskin said to himself, well, there you are. He has twanged a heartstring with that gift; the game starts with a sentimental move. He watched them exchange the knowing glance of old friends.

"I hope you like them, too," Dierker said almost as an afterthought.

"Nice set of books," Baskin said. "Sure I like them."

"They belong at the ranch. You knew it," Kate said, and she kissed Dierker's cheek.

Baskin stifled a scowl and drank an extra glass of wine.

Later when Dierker did address him there seemed to be a slight condescension to it. "So you went up onto a glacier alone, did you?" he said a little loudly. "Packed in, huh? Great! What glacier was it exactly?"

"Slimy Glacier just below Cold Nose Peak."

"Ah, yeah. How many days did you stay up there?"

"He stayed too long," Kate put in. "Show him your bad leg."

"No old wounds, please," Dierker said.

They talked on and on that evening and finally the topic got around to body mysticism. Kate was the exponent and she went on about Ouspensky's experiences with Gurdjieff (Baskin had no idea who either of them were) and she explained how, yes, this was the strain of mysticism which tries to put you more fully into an experience of your body rather than taking you out of the body.

"Norman O. Brown and that sort of thing?" Dierker asked.

"Well, to an extent," she said. "But you know the leading philosopher of my particular cult, don't you?"

"Sarah, I suppose."

"Of course. She could really explain this so that it made great sense. The body as a holy temple, all that. But more: how if you begin to take pleasure in the body's small things life just gets more pleasant."

"Is this a kind of Eastern idea?" Dierker asked. "Wasn't Sarah a student of Zen, I mean, and doesn't this tie in with that?"

"Some, but body mysticism really goes back to Dionysus. She was great on the Greeks, too. And she put it all together, actually, in very American straightforward ways. She wasn't much of a lyricist, as you know, and didn't really think all this had to be explained in religious rhetoric or poetry."

Baskin listened in some disbelief. He thought of Sarah's pantheism and her old celebration of her nakedness, but didn't know about all this and hadn't guessed that she had mystical or philosophical corners. Also, the way Kate and Dierker talked so easily about it put him off again; he knew Sarah best, after all, he wanted to tell them, yet these facts loomed up like sudden large secrets. For the moment he could only be slightly angry with them and he felt Dierker and Kate in unison again and didn't like that either. When they drew him into the conversation, he could only pretend that, yes, sure he knew about Sarah's ideas.

"But she told me when I was very young not to take any of her religious ideas seriously," he added.

"That's because they were too important to be taken seriously," Dierker corrected him.

This made him madder, but he said nothing.

After a while he wanted to get up in protest and go off to bed as he had done with the Neuborns that evening. Yet he couldn't. That would leave Dierker and Kate locked in serious conversation about the body and just wouldn't do. So he sat there. Soon Kate was explaining how she spent her mornings down at the bunkhouse, though, and he perked up again.

"It's where I practice Sarah's crafts," she said. "In this summer heat you get burned out of your mind, but winter's another kind of therapy. You have the sting of the air on your limbs and the slight warmth of the sun—you beg it to get into your pores."

"What do you do exactly?" Dierker wanted to know. "Think deeply?"

She smiled. "No, not really. You practice thinking about nothing. Or you try to get aware of certain parts of your body. You talk to your parts and touch them. Sensation is the antithesis of death, as Sarah put it, so you massage yourself into life."

Baskin's mind went off like a dervish and he visualized that sun deck, the bare boards, the steady noise of the river nearby, and the rhythms of Kate's fingers on herself and inside her. She masturbates, he thought, and even his thought was nearly a stutter, a helpless realization, and he could imagine her writhing there, legs open, slit all sweaty in the sunrays, arms reaching, breasts pulled flat, muscles yawning. Binocular image: that bunkhouse as a shrine to Kate and her striding around in all her fluid rawskinned beauty, hair down, acting as high priestess.

Dierker was entering into the talk with obvious new enthusiasm. He was trying hard to ask the right questions.

"Does all this help the mind?"

"The body *is* the mind," Kate told him. "Sarah knew this. The old dualism about mind and body as separate things just doesn't hold up. All new psychological concepts bring them closer together and what Sarah always understood is that you have to caress and ease them both."

Quickthought: sure, of course that's what Kate does down there every morning before noon. She doesn't write, so there we have it: she plays with herself. Poor thing.

"Must be why I'm so mentally stable," Dierker said. "I play a lot—as you damn well know—and keep myself in good physical shape. A little running, a rubdown, some sunlamp every day or so."

"That's mostly true," Kate said. "Not many great physical specimens have emotional troubles."

"What about me?" Baskin asked. The way they turned and looked at him he wished he hadn't said anything.

"You're never sick, are you?" Kate came back. "So there you are: there's a relationship. You keep your mind sharp and your body keeps itself mostly mended."

"You're even trimming up," Dierker added. "Must have been that trek up the mountain."

"I don't think my m-mind and body talk to each other much," Baskin said, faintly aware of his lie.

"You know better than that," Kate said and she gave him a look which was knowing, but hard to interpret.

He sank away from the conversation again when they started throwing around names of authors, oracles and assorted famous body mystics—things he just hadn't studied. He listened, recording it all, but couldn't participate. He couldn't get up and leave either, so found himself unusually grateful when Dierker announced he was tired and going to bed.

They said their goodnights and Baskin trudged up to his loft. Fluffing his pillow, though, he got worried. The glances at the table, their constant conversation, the evening topic boiled up a jealous mood in him so that he couldn't think of sleeping. Dierker would try and sneak over to Kate's room. He knew it. They've probably done it before, several times, and they won't even have to say a word and disturb me, he reasoned with himself, and he put his shoes back on. Thoughts, thoughts: they're downstairs and I'm up, so I won't hear the footsteps! Besides, be logical: Kate is lying in there raving for a man. Hasn't had one in a year or so, probably, so that all she gets is a little self-manipulation down at the bunkhouse in the sunshine. And Dierker has just hopped a plane—and for what? To see his bastard son who he can't talk to? Forget it.

He crept back downstairs and stationed himself deep in the sofa in the main room, covering himself with the afghan. Dierker would have to cross the darkened room en route to Kate's door. All right. He felt better. Still, he didn't dare sleep and as he lay there he grew suspicious that Dierker might have already crossed over. What then? Or will Kate go to *him?* Or am I hard-hearted and paranoid?

He didn't sleep all night. In the morning, groggy and feeble, he declined to join them for breakfast and staggered back upstairs for some hurried rest. "Body m-mysticism," he whispered to himself as he fell asleep.

Three hours later he bolted upright in bed. Mid-morning at the bunkhouse. Scrambling, he threw on his clothes, descended from the loft, and started across the meadow with an ambush of quickthoughts: they'll be tangled together by now and chanting—the chanting just to throw me off should I happen to show up. Or they're lying there grinning at Mother Nature. He quickened his pace.

But Kate was strolling around the sundeck with her hands thrust in her jeans. Relief swept over Baskin and he managed to ask, "Ha, say, hello there, where's Dierker?" She gestured toward the point of the peninsula at the river's bend and there he was all right, flyrod whipping the morning air in a high arch.

Baskin hated himself for staying so suspicious, but he never left them to themselves. Through the day and evening, weary with distrust, he heard them discuss the body, the mind and assorted metaphysical postulations and he became certain at times that they went at it just for his benefit. "But Huxley said that evolution has come to an end and that the end product is man!" Dierker would point out in a surprising capsule of literary and philosophic information. "Not so, though!" Kate would retort. "Mankind is in a continuing evolution. The environment he's creating for himself now is altering him, for one thing, so that he's having to adapt in almost every physiological and psychological way!" Baskin blinked and nodded and went on listening to all this, wary that they had simply discovered a topic he couldn't talk about and were pushing their advantage. Another way of ignoring me, he decided. And after I'm completely insensible and fall asleep they'll steal off together as I thought they'd do last night.

Determined not to let this happen, he forced himself awake, but another vigil on the sofa that night almost addled him. Once he began to hallucinate and imagined a phosphorescent Dierker gliding through the room toward Kate's neon doorway. Zither music, too. And once he had visions of several old familiar math problems he had once solved which now, suddenly, revealed that he had worked them incorrectly. He struggled up to make a pot of coffee. Then, after the coffee had helped him to stay awake he decided to tiptoe over to Dierker's door and peek inside.

Softly. The door opened a crack for him. The steady drone of Dierker's snore reassured him and since it was nearly morning anyway he crept back to the loft. Sleep, sleep: I need nine hours every night, my usual dreamless hours, he murmured as he settled in.

Dierker's last day came.

The hours filled up with diversions, Dierker's sort of

thing: music blaring from the shortwave all day, a game of gin between Kate and Dierker as the lunch of cold cuts was served, chess between Dierker and Baskin in mid-afternoon—they split two games because, as Baskin saw it, his weariness prevailed—and then some more fishing before dusk. Baskin went down to the river for this final angling with Dierker and in the faint slanting rays of sunlight, mosquitoes gathering around them, he studied his father's profile against the water's shimmer; you're hardly a man without qualities, he found himself thinking, but you're enigmatic. Unknown or unknowable, no matter. So there they stood, silhouetted, faceless in that last glare of the river, darkness coming on. Finally Dierker put away his gear and came over to Baskin and said, "Yeah, listen, I have your money for you. Thanks very much for the loan."

Kate's warning: a strategy, all this.

Dierker took a deep breath as Baskin made a final cast. "This is my last trip out here," he said.

"Well, I'm only staying a few more months myself," Baskin answered. "Then I'll probably never come back."

Silence then. A long pause while Baskin reeled in. From across the river and deep in the woods came an owl's cry which echoed over the stones.

"We had lots of fun here," Dierker began again. "Lots of people came out those first years, you know, and so many of them—well, they had no idea what all this was about. Not really. Your mother was a very deep woman, I mean, and the things she did—oh, not everybody understood why. Not even me. But she had all these ideas—the things Kate and I have been talking about these last few days—and she had this way about her. It's a way you couldn't entirely know about because you had another kind of—well, you were her little boy."

"I knew her awfully well," Baskin said defensively.

"Oh, you did. I know that," Dierker said, but his tone said no, oh no, Baskin, not at all.

Baskin put his gear together and they started back up the footpath toward the ranch. He knew that Dierker was trying to make a speech, some sort of overdue statement, and decided to let him. Darkness hovered; in the last movements of the twilight breeze the pines whispered among themselves. The footpath was narrow, though, so that Baskin had to lead the way and Dierker had to call out his next apology.

"I would have seen a lot more of you both in Chicago and New York if Sarah had let me!" Dierker shouted at Baskin.

"I know she wouldn't let you," Baskin called back.

They kept walking in silence until they reached the top of the river bank and then they started across the meadow. They were in the high wind-waving grass now, pacing slowly toward a lighted window in the distance, quiet, and Baskin could feel his father gathering himself together. Let him get it out, Baskin wished. Let him say some goddamned thing for his own sake.

"Your mother," Dierker said, starting slowly but directly, "was my life's love. Since I can't come out here any longer, my life's mostly ended. Really, that's all I have to tell you." Baskin waited for more, then, but it didn't come; at first the simplicity of Dierker's statement won him, melted him and he felt, oh, why haven't you said it before, years ago? But then he recoiled from his own rush of emotion and felt, ha, what the hell? That makes up for all those years, does it? And so they walked on, silence spreading thick between them.

At the pump in the yard they stopped to wash. Dierker skinned out of his shirt and stood there stocky and robust, a clump of gray hair matting his chest, his sunlamp tan caught in the slanting yellow light of the kitchen window. He dried himself with a towel and said, "To fall in love in the old romantic way—this is my personal opinion—you have to be a real human being. For a while, I mean, when Sarah and I were younger, I wasn't much of a human being, just a prick. She was a human being, but I didn't even notice it I was such a prick. Then later when I was getting all right myself I discovered her, but it was too late. It was always too late and now it's especially too late. Everything completely evaporated. But, hell, you ought to hear some of this."

Baskin dried himself. He couldn't answer, so just stood there trying to weigh and balance all Dierker said. Then a sinking feeling came over him so that he knew he'd resolve this as he had always done with Sarah, with Parmelee, and with everyone else who had reached out clumsily to touch him; he'd play it cool, politely cool, and let it pass.

"You ought to know that I've had a very good life with my family," Dierker went on, leaning against the pump. His mood had turned pensive, so that he seemed to talk only partially to Baskin. "A very good life, but not what your mother had to give. Sarah, you know, offered two things: some excitement and—how shall I say it?—some deep currents. The things Kate and I have been discussing, for instance: a sense of the body and how good life is. The old girl—now this is the irony, I suppose—the old girl didn't have life too easy a lot of times, but she understood *how* happiness could happen, I think, and she taught some of us."

A lengthy pause. Leaning on the pump. Stars overhead.

At their last dinner that evening, then, the three of them listed Sarah's interests and ideas. Between soup and cognac came the catalog of her life: her interests in conservation, natural history, education, nudism, politics, literature (both the hack and the hoity-toity, as she put it), feminism, geology, botany, biology, astronomy, the occult, music. Then things she hated: schools, cities, funeral parlors and morticians, organized religion, war, overcooked meat, desserts. In all this Baskin began to feel a queasy uncertainty, a distrust of the sentimentalities, of the sudden rush of nostalgia and fond remembrance. How should Sarah be regarded? Isn't Dierker inventing the lie we afford the dead and isn't he creating a myth of Sarah now different from that little woman with rolled-down socks, pizza breath and pipe dreams? Guilt and distrust: Baskin felt them both. He was guilty for not having cared enough about Sarah, oh, true, but he distrusted this bath of recollection, too. Keep away from Dierker, a voice told him; listen from afar.

They talked all night, into the next morning, through a breakfast of eggs and more brandy, and on until Dierker had to get ready for the plane coming to pick him up just before noon. Remember and forgive, they seemed to be asking him; know the Sarah we knew, not the one who threw tantrums at your professors, not the one who cursed your growing independence, not the one who hated you for being yourself and who felt you should live your life saying thank you, oh, thanks Mom, for all those hours of tutoring and murder of the spirit. Good Old Sarah: that was what Dierker wanted to sell now, sure, but Sarah had been a woman for whom he had given up nothing; dearest Sarah, good friend, Kate was telling him, but she had known a benevolent patron and so had known only a partial truth.

"Come see me in New York," Dierker said before he got into the little plane that noon. "I mean it, please." He put a hand on Baskin's shoulder and his mouth went slack with sadness when he said it, but, oh, I'm driven to think about everything too much now, Baskin knew; I have to think out Kate just now, I have to remember Sarah in my own way, thank you, and I have to reckon with myself and my stupid gifts and the life coming on.

"We'll see," Baskin answered as the prop roared and his father's pilot waited.

"You make him come," Dierker said to Kate.

"I will," she promised.

"Good-bye, then!"

Good-bye, good-bye, good-bye, good-bye.

ᕗ XIII ᕘ

Baskin started stalking the rooms of the lodge as soon as
Dierker had left. As the hours ticked by, he talked to
himself. An aching dork swinging between my strides.
My eyes being pulled toward the window. Kate down
there on the sundeck. Agony. The inmost disaster and
monstrous hang-up. Besides, it's hot as hell in here; I feel
like I'm in an incubator wanting to be born.

About the second day of this after his father's departure he got a sense of himself and it amused him. This
helped.

He remembered how Burgess once described his first
moment alone with his first girl friend, how he made
elaborate strategies just in order to work up the courage
to hold her hand, how he devised his position and hers,
how he held his breath, looked away, let his hand creep
along through the space between them until ever-so-
lightly their fingers brushed. I'll have to do something
like that now, Baskin decided, but of course matters are
more erotic. Kate is hardly virginal. It's me. And there's a
long electric nerve strung through my silly body, attached here and there at the tip of my dork, up my global

belly, twined around my spine, hitched to my brain, plugged into my eyes, and if any point along the circuit gets overloaded the whole thing goes like a bad fuse. What if I go down to the sundeck and she's naked as morning in the lotus position or whatever she does? There she sits with that lovely brown cunt winking hello and welcome. What do I do? Or she's in a talkative mood, very metaphysical? Or she's full of nags so that the moment I appear she starts fussing about money or about why I went off up the mountain and hurt my leg or about how I should do this or think that? Plan now. Use your remarkable machine and memory bank. Devise. What would Burgess do? Or Dierker? Or a hundred other normal studs? Suppose she's all naked and sunbathing: what then except a gawking retreat? No, I'll have to take off my clothes.

He studied this plan one whole evening, sitting in the loft staring into pure blue space and seeing only the things he conjured himself,

Suppose she's in the buff, okay. I nod casually and start removing my shirt, maybe remarking about how hot the mornings are nowadays, and she's all occupied with her meditations—besides, she went around the ranch with Sarah and god knows who else that way, so why should she pay much attention to my undressing?—and she just lies there, breathing (breasts, oh) and taking the sun. Okay: suppose she's dressed. Blue jeans and shirt. There she sits on the rail gazing at the river, dreaming Hindu symbolisms. Only one possible gesture: I *still* get undressed. I stretch and yawn indifferently, drop my drawers and say, ho me, mind if I sundeck myself? But, all right, she just sits there. "Lie here beside me, my dear," I mutter lewdly, and she unfastens things, all sorts of buttons and clasps, so that denim and linen fall aside and there she is, resplendent, tipped with love dew, and, oh god this'll never work.

Make it happen, though.

Sitting among my old baseball cards plotting sex.

He felt that amusing distance from himself again. One can't be precocious in everything, he decided, and he laughed out loud so that Kate called up from downstairs to ask what was the matter. Nothing, he replied, and he didn't even want to go down; enough that he dreamt the sundecked dreams of time and space, enough that the next morning—weather permitting—he'd go across the meadow like a clockwork sexual commando.

Once again, men, let's go over details. You, Baskin, carry the weapon. Set watches. Everybody have an arsenic capsule in case this fails?

The morning arrived fair and perfect, so soft that Baskin could hear the wildflowers opening and the streams running high in the mountains; he lay deep in his bed aware of his body, each pore and fiber. Dreams of coed lab assistants, waitresses, perfumed classmates, and the photographed young ladies of his old porno collection lingered for a moment in his mind, then he lay awake and waiting. Kate, as usual, stirred below in the kitchen. A long, fretful wait. Then the screen door flapped shut.

He went to the downstairs window in a hurry to see her shape grow smaller down the trail.

At his bath, he went over every detail once more. After having dusted himself with too much powder so that he resembled an albino, he stepped back into the shower and rinsed off again. For ten minutes he pared his fingernails. In jeans, T-shirt, sweater and sandals he went forth.

Halfway there, he stopped to compose himself.

Then the bunkhouse. His footfall on the first step thundered beneath him.

"Hello, mind if I join you?"

"Hi! Of course I don't mind."

She's dressed to the hilt, blue jeaned and sweatered just as I am, he said to himself sadly, but he was on the edge of a towering diving platform, up on his toes, ready, now or never. She gave him an odd look in the sudden silence that lurched between them, but he accomplished most of his mission in one awful daring yank. His jeans fell with a plop to his ankles. Pause. Horrendous passage of time. With some difficulty, then, he stepped out of them, stumbling slightly, grabbing the rail of the sundeck for support. It was then too late for talk and he couldn't have talked anyway, so that he went right into his fumbling strip act without a word, saying, damn, I've blown it already because my face is all terror-stricken, hardly placid as planned, and I think my knees are trembling. Off came the sweater. Unbelievable pause while the river drained itself completely dry. Off came his wisp of a shirt and for the first time ever in his life he noticed that he had a few freckles on his arm. Awkwardly, he stretched out on the bare boards. Hard as hell and hot. Then he remembered his sandals and decided to edge them off his feet without rising. They wouldn't come off. Struggling and almost kicking at himself, he finally managed to catapult one halfway across the deck near Kate's feet; timidly, he unbuckled the remaining one and slipped it off. Great overwhelming pause. Mt. Kintla deflated like a giant balloon and disappeared from his gaze and there he lay knowing a world of gasping truths: that Kate was watching him in a stupefied condition, that his body was no longer bulbous and white but merely rotund and slightly red, that his heart would never last.

The rustle of her clothes broke his mind and he looked up at a clear blue sky, his gaze piercing the stratosphere, the hidden distant stars. Reminder: think about nothing at all or about a mystic part of the body, the liver, say, or the esophagus. She settled beside him, then, and there they lay: side by side, rigid as two planks in the sundeck, not quite touching, and his eyes were tightly closed now, pressed so firmly that they burned in their sockets as he listened to her breathing and the whispered descant of the running river. Then she was laughing.

He was almost sure she was laughing. Disturbed, he refused to move, but after a while he had to raise up to make certain and there she was, sitting up above him, her face in her hands, her soft brown shoulders bumping in hysterical giggles. Then he looked down and saw himself. It rose like a majestic pink icon in the morning sun. Above his scarred and chubby legs and below his healthy belly it rose up to dare the surrounding peaks; it stood up like an idiot intruder, reviling and mocking him, and he cracked a thin smile himself. Then she hovered above him, laughing and saying his name, and her hair fell over his face and shut out his history, his clusters, and the rest of the world.

❧ XIV ❦

———————

"If you make love in the same place twice it's as awful as being married," she told him, so they did it everywhere: in the window seat, in the loft, three or four places around the bunkhouse, in the forest, at the stables (upright and in a stall, though she protested and didn't know why), and on top of Sarah's desk in the reading room. Also, an assortment of styles accompanied this tour and he learned from her in those next weeks the pleasures of the roving kiss and bite, various upside-down deliveries and mouthings, and a few calesthenic assaults.

"Teach me something else today," he would say.

"You know too much already," she'd answer cynically. "You must have ten thousand new clusters in your brain."

"I've lost count of my clusters."

"Good. I'm glad."

Up a mountain trail they went, picnic basket filled with a lunch they would only half devour. Into her bedroom she led him, ostensibly to help spread the covers and make the bed. In the bath they showered together, she explained, to save the precious hot water.

A honeymoon period.

When they managed to disengage themselves they even talked.

"What were you dreaming?" she asked him one morning as they roused themselves out of their deep sleep. They sprawled in the big downstairs bed, her leg thrown over his.

"Huh, what?"

"I asked what you were dreaming."

"Nothing," he mumbled, burrowing into his pillow. "I never dream."

"Never dream? What do you see when you sleep, then?"

"A field of gray."

"Everyone dreams. So do you."

He watched her with one eye while he burrowed down. "N-not at all," he protested. "I've never dreamed. It's one of my secret weapons. When I sleeps I sleeps a sleepy sleep."

She sat up in bed to lecture him. Everyone dreams, she explained, and so did he; only some deep sleepers don't remember their dreams or the act of waking makes them forget. "You ought to get interested in your dream life, Baskin, I mean it. It'll be a whole new world for you."

So he started trying to remember and retain his dream life and sure enough there it was: little dramas unfolded in his slumber and behind his eyes in a strange parade of fantasy came Burgess, Kate, Sarah, Weihmeyer, and all the untouchable maidens of the Midwest.

He told Kate his dreams at breakfast. New corridors everywhere. In one dream he played tennis singles with Lothridge while looking on stood the various Nobel Laureates from the school, Millikan and Compton and Fermi and the others. In another he tried to work in his carrel, but a force of workmen insisted on building windows in each of the four walls. In a brief vignette a bear chased him down Quartz Creek and when he turned to fight the bear had turned into another Baskin, one replete with Sarah's baggy socks and grinning stupidly.

"All surface stuff. You're just not very complicated," Kate informed him.

"Hell, I'm full of hidden meanings," he argued.

During the days a new energy coursed through him. Gathering and hauling flat rocks from the river's edge, he started constructing a stone walkway between the lodge and the nearby outbuildings. In his plan he foresaw a whole network of lovely walks through a flowery formal garden, the paths of Eden, and as he melted the extra pounds from his body and hardened himself in this endless work he envisioned the ranch made over into a landscaped retreat where great scholars and thinkers would gather. At times he worked naked, his body growing slimy with perspiration. Kate brought bags of cement from Columbia Falls and he kept on the job, mixing and pouring, laying the rock, his mind neutralized by labor.

At night they went together into the kitchen and cooked. Learning new recipes, they experimented in spices and herbs and curries; gravies and sauces began to simmer constantly on the back burners of the stove and puffy desserts flowered in the oven, yet no matter how much he ate Baskin seemed to keep trim. A sudden new metabolism took hold of him.

Typical day. Nuzzling each other awake for twenty minutes or so around mid-morning. Breakfast eggs with a pitcher of juice, then Kate at the bunkhouse while Baskin tugs at the stones. Very sweaty. A kiss in the meadow as Kate, fatigued with reading and meditations, comes toward the lodge and as Baskin, arm-heavy, gives up and starts toward the bunkhouse. A small lunch, just a salad and beer. A salty afternoon kiss in the shade of the porch, Baskin's rough hand traveling down her spine to cup her sweet bum, her fingers tracing his frontside contours. A naked river stroll. Quick into the bushes while two earnest Boy Scouts float softly by in their canoe. Beads of perspiration at Kate's temples. Another haul of flat rocks huffed and puffed from the riverside, a new batch of cement. A mid-afternoon shower, then a moment in the window seat or in an overstuffed chair or at a small footstool which tests and grades sexual creativity; Kate's thighs not-so-daintily thrown over his shoulders or encasing his ribs or finding new ways to open. Talk afterwards —immediate or distant subjects such as Sarah or the sadness of history, newspaper items or the metaphysical pulse of the new decade—and the evening. A large meal and the civilized ritual of dining. Music on the shortwave, Kate tidying the kitchen, Baskin tending the horses and chopping wood. More talk, murmurs of all the evenings of their lives up until now. A game of gin or chess, Baskin explaining Paul Morphy's style of play and a famous game or two. Mountains outside whispering among themselves in the darkness. The inevitable weather report: cooler. Naked in the bathroom together with Kate padding around like a lioness, musty with the smell of sex through her perfume. The myrrh of cunt. Putting off the day, stretching it with a last topic or two as if everything might not get said. Then to bed and his weary dear member suddenly in her mouth, the milky way exploding, the cosmos expanding, her fingers guiding him in again, the last of the day's energies going. Slumber. Dreams mostly still unremembered because they were unnecessary because life was a dream itself. Deeper dreams with dark shapes. The nuzzling once more at mid-morning.

At times, things she said pinned themselves in his head.

"I swore I'd take my body out of circulation permanently, but then here you were. A woman's body is nothing more than currency on the job market, I told myself, and I couldn't afford to spend it, but then here I was feeling so much about you, asking myself what it was about you that made me feel it. Your innocence? What?"

Or: "That night at the Addison place when we were stuck—I thought it would happen right then. But you never made a move."

Or: "I like to see you chop wood with your shirt off like this. Your body's getting hard, you know."

It was suddenly September, true, and new rhythms had started in his body so that he moved with a new pace, without his old herky-jerky clumsiness. His biceps had knotted, his belly had flattened, his stutter seldom came. The walkway now curled from the back door to the smokehouse to the stables and in order to lay the rest of it he had to sweep away the first snow. Firewood stacked up by the porch. Also, as winter came on, the hired hands drifted back, standing in the yard with their hats in their hands, nodding, and Baskin sent the horses with them across the mountains to the west where the weather of the next months would be less severe. "No, we won't be needing you this year," he told them, and he wrote out expense checks for them and paid for the horses' care on the western slopes.

September. The air bristled with cold and he looked forward to the first heavy snow, to a morning when they would wake up and find themselves buried in it, the roads closed again, shut off like the burning hermits they were. In preparation, they made several trips down to West Glacier, Columbia Falls and the Polebridge Store putting in supplies. Kate locked up the bunkhouse for the winter and started her morning meditations in front of the large bay window, sprawling on the rug with her books and papers so that Baskin remembered himself there; a kind of security took over, now, with the house shutting out the north wind which came down the valley, the hearth lit, Kate's presence felt everywhere.

They went deeper into Sarah's things. A sprig of bear-grass stuffed into a book. A grocery memo. Another line written across a bookmarker which made them curious: "Art is a bone thrown to us by reality to keep us from barking." Sarah's or someone else's? The deck of Tarot cards.

"Of course she didn't believe in these," Kate said. Then, less certain: "Not exactly, anyway."

"Did you have your fortune told with them?"

"Lots of times."

He grinned. "A new fortune every day or so?"

"Well, it was something to do. No harm. We did it lots when the weather got bad."

"Could you do mine?"

"With help. I have the book here someplace that ex-plains all the cards and combinations."

He found the book for her and they sat cross-legged on the rug before the fire. Key cards flew everywhere. He was the Magician. The Hierophant crossed him. The Hanged Man lay ahead of him and the Jester behind him —which made him think of Dierker. The general prospect was favorable, yet he watched Kate's eyes as she read the passages in the book which explained all these things and she was dead earnest; she's not a very good con woman, he decided, because she doesn't elaborate on any of this. Very little show biz about her. Serious.

"I can't imagine Sarah diddling with this kind of thing," he said, deliberately trying to stir her up.

"Sarah was interested in lots of kinds of mysticism and

symbology," she answered. Kate was strangely pensive and sad. "I got the feeling about Sarah," she went on, "that she just didn't trust words very much. Perhaps wrote as she did—the trite, hack work—because she didn't believe words could say much very important about how we live. But nature had a language all its own to her. And there were basic, almost mythic truths."

Baskin didn't know what to say, so just smiled and remarked, "Did you find any of those truths in all the readings she gave you with this deck of cards?"

"My fortune was always lousy," she said. "Death and the King and all the grim ones."

She seemed so serious that he reached over and took her hand. When they kissed, then, she held on so tightly that he smiled and whispered, "Hey, there, what's the matter?" But she didn't answer.

≫ XV ≪

He liked to think of himself that autumn as an ordinary man. A luxury, that thought. A thousand small vanities lived in it.

These are my hands, he could muse, and they're all hard; this is my land for looking; this is my dork for love-strokes; this walkway is my simple pride; this woman mirrors my heart. Such simplicities made his thoughts fly backward into realization, into the knowledge that his former achievements in Chicago, New York, New Orleans and in all those productive years had given him only a superficial sense of himself. He knew what he had felt there on the lagoon in Audubon Park, that miasma of weary doom, that feeling that he had come to the end of things. If I hadn't come here, he admitted, I'd have gone on working my equations, doing speed tricks for my colleagues and worshipping students, until I had become, at best, a fool and at worst a psychotic. Split from the world, schizophrenic, muddled, lost. I would have gone out onto the lagoon for a stroll one day. Girls in bathing suits lounging on towels and blankets, so distant and lovely that I couldn't bring myself to stare and yet couldn't look away. Repressions bombarding me. My work back at the cubicle beckoning, calling me, saying, Come Sit Here Where You Belong, Where Existence Is Not a Dream. I would have gone slowly around the lagoon, a fragrance of summer spiraling my thoughts away. Hateful Sarah on my mind. Other painful visions, too: those New York movie houses, all dark and faintly smelling of popcorn and urine, where I fondled myself as some coy plaything writhed in technicolor; my room all piled with paperbacks and with phonograph albums to remind me of my abandoned musical flirtations; the solitary seat which I occupied in Yankee Stadium or at Shea where I watched those indifferent games and wondered why baseball wasn't the same for me. Strolling that lagoon I would have reached the curved bridge, looked down at my rippled reflection on the water, looked away, would have glimpsed the empty cells of my computered life, and they would have found me there among the lilies, bloated with water and discontent, a shoe missing, my eyes gone to the goldfish, my brain a sponge of sad little numbers.

No good, all that. I am an ordinary man. Feed me, laugh, fuck me, make small talk, I am into the life Sarah taught me to escape. Or did she? Did she plan all this, too? Has she charted my emotional journey out?

As he thought about his luck—this luck of having, suddenly, the pleasant and almost forgotten normalcies of existence—and as he saw himself as an ordinary sexual, energetic, physical young man touring an old paradise, it also pleased him to think of Kate as an extraordinary woman. Her body, for one thing. She had those two perfect dimples at each side of her spine above her lovely ass; her face was pretty with a nice wide mouth for wet kisses, and deep eyes, all lovely and timeless, her breasts were enormous with high, jutting nipples; her rib cage was pronounced, her waist slim, her thighs hard and brown, her ankles long, her feet narrow and curved; the pocket of her sex was small and rugged and hairy. But more than this. Her frankness appealed to him, her worldliness, her raw self; if he was up tight, she could wing it. She knew men and women, money, the reasons that lay behind the reasons people gave, the pulse of the age. He liked the little things she did to shock him out of his old self—how she sat on the toilet, for instance, with the door open or how she made him tell his dreams or talk about himself or how—when she was ready—she took his hand and put it between her legs so that he felt her all wet and open.

She's one alone, a solitaire, nothing like her, he told himself, yet that autumn he detected their small change and evolution at the ranch. All wasn't right. As sure as the trickle on the rock high in the mountains erodes and wears away the stone until the avalanche begins, all wasn't right.

She was a poor writer, he decided. Worse than Sarah— or, perhaps, slightly better so that she knew too much to turn out the stuff Sarah wrote yet not significantly better. When the winter weather brought her up from the bunk-house, he could see her habits there on the floor of the main room. Unlike his mother who would peck away at the typewriter and pile up those pages—virtually the same chapters over and over—Kate would dawdle and scribble out something longhand, erase, modify, rip it up and start again.

"What're you writing?" he'd ask, simply.

"An essay, I think," she'd say. "Maybe a novel. I don't know what it might be."

"What's it about?"

"I'm not sure. I'll show it to you later."

She never showed him anything.

Also, deeper than this, some uncertainties crowded her. She wanted to prepare, she claimed, to return downworld again and be part of the cities, yet she also clung to this place, the safety of it, and Baskin knew that she never wanted to leave. She also wanted sex—more than even I do, he began to realize—but she sometimes seemed to hate the escape and recreation and overbearing euphoria of it. She pleased herself by startling and confounding and teasing him with sex—especially the sudden unexpected mouthings and turnings when his appetite for her was so strong that all the familiar and straightforward techniques would have done just as well. Yet their tumbling, he knew, was only an interlude for her, a postponement of another growing mood. "Damn, you're good at this," he'd say to her in the midst of it, and she'd say, "I know it. It's part of my curse. All talent is a curse." And he'd know that she meant it, that she wanted something more than this sway and lovely plunge of hips.

"What else?" he'd ask, trying to be helpful. "What is it you want?"

Gazing out at the light snow peppering down, she wouldn't answer.

By October he had resorted to clowning. At his old blackboard set up in the reading room, he mimicked Dr. Ludmiller, who was always a victim of a thick accent and nearsightedness. "Vat's dis, shtudents? Tell me, qvick, somebody! Vat's dis movement in our equation mean? Huh? Oh, I see: das ist just un imperfection on ze blackboard! Sorry, pleeze." The result: Kate's momentary laughter and appreciation, no lasting change of temperament. He tried smoking an old briar pipe. No response. A scrap of ribbon tied on the end of his weary dork, white for surrender, got only a smirk and a "Baskin, really." Unless he waited three or more days between times they made love she moved with merely an automatic resignation. The honeyed rhythms of the house slowed down.

Conversation: it was a bit too civilized for his taste, but there was plenty of it.

Kate talked about the war, the never-ending war in Asia, and, yes, it has to be stopped, all wars have to end, and can't we build a computer, she wondered, which programs what's right for everybody so there won't be any politics or any greed or inequity involved? He told her yes, sure, Norbert Wiener was working at that, applying cybernetics to social science and neurophysiology and psychology. Old clusters rose up in his mind: blocks of information which he gave her to consider. And can't we learn how to live, she asked him, and do we have to build cities that kill us? And he talked about Wittgenstein and Dubos and sometimes in the midst of her speculations he would set off into his own; he would talk about radionuclides or he'd tell her about one of his experiments at the Argonne National Lab where he worked a few times, how they found that the "noble gases," so-called in the belief that they didn't react with other substances, were not really inert.

"Too technical," she'd say to him at these times. "That's not what I was talking about." And off they'd go in another direction.

He noticed that her categories grew larger and larger and sometimes fell off into the mystical or metaphysical while his always shrank smaller as they talked. He would begin telling her about some of his radiochemical studies, how he had learned to measure fission products and what they spent their days doing at the Fermi Institute and at the New York center, but she would turn the talk around. Once he even sprang to the blackboard and began illus-

154

trating his point with an equation, but he turned, embarrassed, to catch her bewildered and disinterested stare. She's not Sarah, he had to remind himself, so let this go.

They each had phone calls in early October, hers from her former husband who had a new job offer and his from Parmelee. Both brought on mild quarrels. "I thought you'd dumped him," Baskin argued. "How the hell does he just ring up like this if that's so?" With Kate it was a clear case of jealousy, too. "You've got something to *do,*" she told him. "That's why there's no damned urgency about you right now! You can walk out of here and go to New Orleans or some neat place like that and start doing your important work again!" He asked her what difference that made and she said, "It makes it unfair between us. Don't you understand? You're taking a little time out for love, but I can't. I just can't!"

He didn't understand at all. He stood alone out at the stable and thought about Parmelee's valuable friendship. The young female instructors Parmelee had provided him: he tried to recall a name, but couldn't. The supper party at the lake. The poor farewell at the airport. In spite of what Kate felt, he enjoyed getting the call and being remembered.

Something else: he was mostly aesthetic, she was mostly not. This conclusion came hard for him because he wanted Kate to be a writer—if that's what she wants, sure—yet she didn't seem to enjoy writing for itself alone; she wanted a craft only to get to something else—what, what?—and not for itself. Watching her exasperation, he could ruminate on himself, could say, yes, that's why I moved out into pure mathematics and theory: because I enjoy playing with numbers, building symmetries, doing my equations whether or not they seem a part of a particular physical or social problem. But not Kate. She wants to address the world directly. She wants to change things, I suppose, herself included; she wants words with a social consequence, activity that leads to some greater significance, a life that leads to meaning. Painful, her struggle. She took up Zen once, she confided to him, but couldn't achieve the level of meditation and grace Sarah seemed to get out of its contemplative practice. "We read these books," she explained, "and I thought I understood it, but it just didn't work for me." Zen, he wanted to tell her, isn't like that, though. You don't go through the disciplines in order to *get somewhere* or *know something* you didn't have before. Zen discipline is its own reason for being; one practices it for itself, because done for its own sake it supposedly unifies one's life. (He remembered all this from the leftover clusters of Sarah's religious instruction, from the books by Noss his mother had made him read, from the little pamphlets on world faiths that used to lie around the house.)

Kate is an extraordinary woman, he told himself. He didn't much want to consider otherwise.

When the first major snowstorm came in mid-October, Kate fell into a solid week of melancholy. Since she didn't want to make love, he finally said, "Hell, you're indulging yourself. Snap out of it."

"Superior people don't let themselves do this: is that what you mean?"

"Yeah, right. You know how Sarah felt about it. So do I."

"Well, cram that."

"What do you mean?"

"You can go around repressing your low moods, but not me. It isn't mentally healthy. I believe in blowing off steam when I'm mad and I believe in getting the doldrums when I'm sad and you can shove it."

"Sarah always said that—"

"Forget what Sarah said! She had her moods, too, believe me. I suppose you're superman, though, and you don't despair of anything."

"If I see a bad cloud coming, I try to head it off. No use getting into it. Besides, it's an indulgence like all introspection and all—"

"I *know* your mother's philosophy. Pity it didn't work with her. She was an open wound."

"Well, I think you ought to snap out of it. I think the weather has you down—winter does that sometimes."

"Unless you happen to be a genius?"

"Wittgenstein was a young mathematician," he told her. "He solved almost every major problem of his time, then he threw it all over and became a gardener for a while. Years later he emerged again and became a philosopher. He had come to the end of something, but it didn't blow his life. He just changed himself. That's what I'm doing now. When I was down in New Orleans I began to feel—"

"Yes, I know, you told me: the sensitive young man coming to grips and all that. I don't want to hear it again."

"Well, hell, let's not fight. All I said was that you should snap out of it."

"Well, I said cram it."

"Don't be a bitch."

"You can shove that, too."

Things definitely altered. Baskin began wondering if Kate moved on some mysterious tide and change of the moon, turning and spinning in orbit around a set of distant moods. At times she spat herself at him; at other times she spun a gossamer film around him, enveloping him with a tangled web of soft phrases and kisses, opening herself to him, snaring his senses. Not long after this argument they went walking in the snow up on the ridge. Dressed in their heavy mackinaws and boots and canvas hunting clothes, they crunched along beneath the snow-laden limbs; a haze of sunlight had appeared, just enough to cast their shadows downhill, but it was bitterly cold. They stopped to watch a young spike buck and an old doe across a ravine, then turned up toward the top of the ridge where the forest thickened and scarcely admitted the sun. Since the argument they had covered a range of subjects, talking as always, but hadn't made love; now, strangely, Baskin knew that Kate was searching for a particular spot. Something. His senses quickened as he moved behind her along an ice-crusted path under the pines. She turned into his kiss, then, and they were inside of each other's coats, tugging and caressing, and his belt and front were suddenly open so that she had him in her fingers, saying, "I just can't wait any longer," whispering so that their breath made them hot and insulated under the mackinaws, and she moved his back against the tree and freed herself, her mouth on his, stroking him until he bulged and pressed against her; a rustle of canvas clothes, then, and she was warmskinned on him, and he found that she had chosen a particular tree with a low branch so that she could take a foothold there, wrapping one eager ankle behind his leg and parting herself and gripping him with her thighs, being his love spider all here and there over him, guiding him into that soft web. He laughed a helpless, thankful laugh.

Later at the lodge she crossed the room naked in the firelight to nestle beside him, saying, "Listen, I'm sorry. I don't know how to say this. Especially after what I did to you this afternoon. It's embarrassing and I'm ashamed of myself, I mean."

"What?" he said, rousing himself from his drowsy and pleasant fatigue there on the hearth rug. "What's the matter?"

"I just want some more. Are you able?"

With a display of happy tact he tried to explain to her that he was.

❧ XVI ❧

But it wasn't always like this.

Their private equations weren't simple, but by November they could dimly comprehend them: Baskin was moving from one life to another and so was Kate. His prodigy years gone, he had entered some erotic latitudes and he was passing on. Kate's identity was perhaps evolving into something like Sarah's: a complex of earth and air, a life somehow more rarefied—though exactly what she didn't know. So as Baskin's change made him smile and lust and feel alive, Kate's took on those different orbits, moods of bitchiness and soft meditation, of disgruntled solitude and self-appraisal and sudden lovemaking.

When she was unresponsive, Baskin caught himself thinking too much about himself again. But what was there to do? Now take me, now don't: who could live with that sort of woman? It drove back into his stockpile of clusters, into memory and wistful daydreaming.

Extraordinary intelligence. What do I do with it? Here it is, a natural phenomenon trained and ready, a computer programmed for what? Of course Lothridge was right: I should search out new relationships and new orders. My education has only introduced me to what we don't yet know and so there's plenty to discover: how the brain really works, how the cell works, what the life of the body really is. Or the limits of the universe, if any. My astronomical musings. $T = 3°K$, then $\lambda\, max = 0.1\ cm$ so that radiation at this temperature, yes, is in the form of radio waves and no other known astronomical source, yes, will contribute significantly to radiation in these wavelengths. Outer space and inner space: it's all there for me and I could hone my thoughts, sure, so that I'm like Einstein, capable of tossing up equations like toys, playfully, and letting them fall and deciphering the order. Making poems out of numbers and concepts, being a god of thought, free and creative. Does one have an obligation? There's a line of thought: to whom do I now owe my intelligence? Even deeper moral questions loom up: do I have the right to dream myself away in the arms of a woman, to spend my energies with her and use myself up, to give away a sudden one hundred IQ points in the animal orgasm of a personal life? Is it my duty to burrow down, to wrap my cubicle around myself, to seek the sullen madness of further genius? For that's what it was, Sarah, whether you knew it or not: you were driving me insane, all the more so because my dear professors and colleagues applauded it. What to do? What to be?

Education. Of course you knew there was only one good way of education, Sarah: your fierce, loving, brutal tutorial style. I couldn't have learned alone, not really, and mass education would have smashed me. In between, there was our combat. The truth is, you had to want me to learn more than I wanted knowledge for myself; like everyone, I was dimmed by natural laziness and wanted to play or squander myself in some happy fairyland of the mind, screwing off, piddling at the piano or thinking of my next hamburger or sprawling like a dullard cub on the grass in our meadow. You had to be there reading me, testing my stress and tolerance, setting my goals always a little beyond my reach. Very early you had the right idea, too, saying, "Shit, Baskin, you be the teacher for a while. Help me with this. Am I supposed to learn quantum theory? Here, read Planck for yourself and then you tell me what the hell's going on, okay? Let me get back to writing this silly book of mine or we won't get new winter coats this year, I guarantee you that!" And it worked. You sat there nodding and looking studious while I explained and condescended to *you* and, ah, the joy of it! Biographies of Galileo, Newton, Leibniz, Einstein, Oppenheimer: oh, remember how we read their lives (or pieced them together where our sources lagged) and tried to decide their emotional states just *before* they made their big breakthroughs? Remember the essay you assigned? "The Acceleration of Scientific Knowledge, 1940–50." And recall the metaphor I used, the one you loved so much about how our accumulated knowledge compared to a falling celestial body constantly quadrupling its speed as it approached a giant magnetic mass?

Knowledge: oh, no doubt of it, its acquisition has a relationship to love, just as love has a relationship to captivity. One must be possessed in order to possess. My mind was in your hands, Sarah love, and you were expertly jacking it off, pounding the right answer until it came up and out, spurting hot, and I could say, "There, Mama, how's that? Is that good for you, too, Mama? S'that whatcha want?" And you were (listen, don't mothers masturbate their boy children in some primitive society trampled by one of our plump lady anthropologists?) buggering me with information, too: stuffing it in all my openings like castor oil and following it with a tablespoon

162

of Jell-O pudding or chocolate cake to get rid of the bad taste of it. My baggy-socked oedipal terror and tutor, my wonder and dream, my mater, love and good riddance.

Short memories of Sarah. Sitting here in this room, your reading room and writing parlor, remembrances come skimming back in the half light, the florist bill you ran up while we were in Chicago, for instance, because we had to have tufts of flowers and fern around that dowdy Kimbark Avenue layout, or the books on that shelf by the telephone table. Authors famous and strange, brown and fair: Herbert Kuhn, Sigmund Freud, Dante Alighieri, John Yount, René Dubos, Bernard Fall, and thirty disparate others (for by that time we had no reading plan) just sitting there to be picked up en route to the toilet. All my pornography kept and read at school, Sarah, yes, and in your house I read the great minds while doing my morning duty.

That green dress. "Throw that damned thing out, won't you?" I said, and you looked surprised and replied, "Oh, hon, you don't like this?" and I said, "You've *had* it ten years or more!" so you walked right over to the kitchen trash pail and dumped it and that was that. I felt bad about it.

"Minnie Minoso eats all his cereal, I'll bet," you told me once, and I had you there and told you, "He's only batting .247 right now and they're talking about trading him." End of vignette.

Sarah: "I got a little constipation, hon, so what do you think I should do?"

Baskin: "Damn, Mama, don't ask me things like that!"

Sarah: "Oh, come on, I was just making talk. You're not interested in whether I'm sick or healthy?"

Baskin: "Okay, right, I'm sorry. You know the bookcase on the way to the bathroom in there?"

Sarah: "Sure I know it."

Baskin: "Okay, pick up the old novel by Daphne du Maurier. Books by women writers give me the shits, so maybe they'll do the same for you."

Places traveled, things done, sure, they all come back and the past changes itself, doesn't it, just as the present shifts around so that we are always trying to find ourselves in it? My memory holds you fixed like a photograph down at Key West or at Stratford-Upon-Avon or in the Edwardian Room of the Plaza or in the saddle up above this ranch, but you don't really stay put so easily. The mind is a silly wheel inside the wheel of time, a bad gyroscope, forgetful or, like me, the awkward rememberer of too much.

Winter.

Days passed with his thoughts on all this and at times he asked Kate to fill in the gaps of his memory, to reflect with him, and she did or didn't according to her mood.

"Sarah loved you, sure, I've told you that. There was hardly anything else on her mind."

"But you admitted something else: I was a projection of Sarah, too, wasn't I? She thought of me as a growth on her own body, I'll bet."

"Not exactly like that."

"She used my intelligence to justify what went on with Dierker, too, didn't she? It was her way of saying, look here: it looked like a big mistake, but see what happened. She used me to justify half her life."

"Maybe so, Baskin, I don't know. What do you want me to say?"

"Oh, nothing. I was just thinking about her again."

On the first day of November a snowstorm blew across the ridge and engulfed them. Baskin got a call from Sonderson, a neighbor, asking if he'd help clear the road by driving one of the snow dozers, so he went out to help.

He worked all day, but the snow kept coming so that it was useless. That evening, exhausted, he trudged back down to the lodge with his snowshoes, fell into a chair, and asked Kate for a drink. What followed was a series of posturings and petty arguments, so many that he lost track of the subjects.

They argued over the contents of the cupboard. Too many canned beans and potatoes, she scolded him. Didn't he have any sense about buying a balanced diet when he went down to the stores?

They argued over the fact that one of her snowshoes had a broken strap.

They argued over Vladimir Nabokov. Except for his autobiography, Kate said, he was phony as hell. "I've only read two of his novels," Baskin countered, but she kept on.

Finally, everything got around to her pet subject: the subjugation of women. "I've had enough of that," he snapped at her. "Women are bullies. Very early in life they find their power: they discover they have a sexual magnetism, something the little boys want and dream about, and they use that prowess like a club. Young boys have to wait years to find their p-power out in the world of c-commerce and competition and once they get it the little girls hate them for it. Hell, if there's anything I'm learning up here with you it's that even a goddamned utopia is a battlefield."

"You're horrible," she spat back at him. "Just like Sarah said! You're just spoiled and rotten and cold and don't give a big damn!"

"Oh, hell, I'm tired. Why are we arguing? Get me a drink, please, Kate, and let's quit this."

"Get your own drink. I'm supposed to be your servant? Is that how we resolve this little discussion?"

The next day he went back out on the road with his

neighbors. The snow had stopped and they had a pleasant morning—with the exception of one disgruntled scholar who complained of a headache and went back to his cabin on Tepee Creek—and one of the wives brought them hot soup and sandwiches at noon. Baskin's back throbbed from bending over the gears of his dozer, but he didn't mind. Let it hurt, he told himself, and take my mind off things; let it be like my trip to the glacier, a small torture and therapy. That afternoon they reached the Polebridge Store where they met another work crew from West Glacier, so the road was cleared and they all had a few beers. "You're all right," one of the men said, gently slapping Baskin's shoulder as they stood around inside the warm store. "Is it true you're a genius or something like that, though?" It was one of those awkward moments—people didn't know how to talk to him, ever— and the man's tone seemed to mean, oh, sorry, you're a poor freak or a cripple, aren't you?

"I think I'm too smart to spend another morning on that dozer," Baskin managed, and the men laughed. It was all right, just fine, and he felt at ease with them and sorry when they were all slightly drunk and decided to go home.

That evening the arguments with Kate were, in order:

The soup. He made the mistake of saying that they had eaten some nice soup earlier in the day out on the road.

The Jeep and the station wagon. "We'll be lucky if either one of them holds up through spring," she insisted.

The academic world. Baskin proposed, like Henry Adams, that no one could possibly get a good education in a regular university curriculum, and Kate told him that he was a pompous idiot. She was considering going to work on her doctorate someplace. He was an exception to the system, yes, but didn't know what he was talking about. Narrow, she called him.

Lovemaking. He said he was damned tired and so she accused him of not caring for her needs and what, she asked, did you really do all day? Amazed at this, he showed her the blisters on his right palm from handling the gears on the snow dozer. When the fuss went on, he said, okay, let's go to bed, it suits me, but she said no I'm not in the mood thank you very much.

Early the next morning he set off in the Jeep for West Glacier. He had in mind a bar there, one of those log cabin retreats with moose and elk heads stuck up dumbly on the walls among the beer advertisements. Also, he mused, I'll shop around in the general store and buy some liquor and have the Jeep checked over. A day in town. He went along at a steady pace, silence of winter all around, and when the sun broke out he took off the Jeep's cover, pulled down his stocking cap and tightened his muffler, and rode along in the brisk air.

Lingering in the stores, he bought himself a new creel for the early spring fishing, some flannel shirts, underwear. There were few people in town, mostly just the rangers and their families and the relaxed storekeepers, but by noon a few winter travelers had stopped in and the restaurant was half filled. As he ate a chicken-fried steak and watery mashed potatoes, he wished Kate were there; the local newspaper had only a few items of international news, mostly high school events and scraps of interest out of Glacier Park, but he read everything, even the classifieds, while he drank three cups of weak coffee. With a sigh, he adjourned to the bar.

There stood the barmaid, sturdy and red-cheeked, a woman of about fifty who said hello out of the side of her mouth; with her, the only occupants of the stools, were two surprisingly pretty girls, about my age, Baskin quickly decided, who were drinking gin and smiling. The four of them sat talking politely, asking about each other. When Baskin said he was a scientist (he knew the term had a slight poetic lilt to it) the girl with short blond hair said, "Oh, groovy, I believe *that*." And the three women laughed and exchanged looks while he insisted it was so.

"What do you do, Pam and Carla?" he asked, pronouncing their names carefully.

"We travel around," Pam, the blond, said.

The other giggled and tossed off her drink.

"Camping out?"

"Sure, we do a little camping."

"We have a camper trailer up at Apgar campgrounds. Come up and see us later."

More giggling. They smelled faintly of smoke, as if they'd been standing around an open campfire. During the next round of drinks, they unbuttoned their jackets and he stole a quick look at their figures. An invitation. Why not? His projections gathered: a phone call to Kate about road conditions, staying down here, small ambiguous excuses.

"You college girls?"

More exchanges of glances. "Oh, we definitely used to be," Carla said, and the gentle mocking tone, already established, continued. The barmaid clung close to them, leaning her elbows across the bar and listening.

"But now you're just traveling around?" he repeated.

"Gathering experience," Pam said, and they broke into laughter.

"You can't get a position without experience," the barmaid added, and this broke them up.

"Buy another round, okay?" Carla laughed and put a hand on his. Very warm. Scalding. He paid for two gins and his beer.

They'd been to Mexico, Florida, across the Arizona desert, up California along the ocean, into Canada, and now back down; in their fleeting descriptions of all this he felt his breath shorten and his neck tingle and he was feeling, oh, two birds flying, two laughing dreamers like the coeds who passed on the campus walks. They were both thin as willows, perhaps younger than he had originally thought, and they tossed off straight gin with a silly abandon that didn't seem to make them particularly drunk. "You come up to the campgrounds and visit," Pam added again as they talked, and he said yes, all right.

Outside the bar they stood in the cold wind beside his Jeep and the girls' car, huddled together, giggles breaking out of them, and Pam—or was it Carla?—asked if he could spend the night. Imagination split his head: the little aluminum camper off nestled in the pines, the three of them in a tangle of blankets and torso, winding and biting on each other, one here, one there, hands everywhere.

"There's room for me?" he asked dumbly.

More laughter. "You could sleep in our car."

"We'll make arrangements."

They slipped into happy vulgarity, their arms laced. "Or you could sleep with Pam because I'm a sport or you could sleep with me because Pam's a sport, okay? Aren't you a sport, Pammy?" Sniggles and hands over their mouths.

"I'm not totally a sport."

"She says she isn't totally."

"We could all sleep together," he heard himself say.

"Oh, what a groove. Hear what he said, Carla?"

"Definitely. I heard it."

"What kind of girls you think we are?"

Burst of nervous laughter. Pam's hand slipped inside his coat.

"We could make the sacrifice, though, couldn't we, Pammy?"

"We've sacrificed before!"

"You two do this all the time, eh?"

"We're travelers in this weary land, Baskin, and our hearts are on the wing."

"Beautiful."

"I wish I'd said that."

They made arrangements. Carla asked him to give them twenty minutes or so. "You know where the campground is," she said. "We want to get ready for you. Okay?"

"How'll I find you?"

"We're the only campers! You think this is vacation time? That campground is empty as anything! All to ourselves."

"See you in a few m-minutes, then."

"You stutter, Baskin love?"

"Sometimes."

"You hear that, Carla, how he stutters?"

He went back inside the tavern to buy a case of beer for the ranch, but having done it wished he hadn't because during the night it would probably freeze in the Jeep. Worrying over this, he also pondered whether or not to call Kate. No, definitely no, perhaps later if all works out.

After wrapping the case of beer in a blanket and putting it into the back of the Jeep, he started off for the campground bristling with excitement and concocting pictures for himself: naked Pam throwing off her flannel nightdress, Carla in lace panties sprawling over him, all of them slimy with heat as they labored. The girls downworld: ah, they're certainly there. Aquarius has dawned and they're all free and winging, scanning the beaches and woods for me, locking their dreams and mine; for a moment he thought about life after the year at the ranch was finished. City apartments. The girl across the hall. Those ever-present lab assistants. Exotic fruits of travel: tall and Swedish, brown islanders, small orientals.

The Apgar campground was shut with a sign that read, simply, CLOSED FOR THE SEASON. Of course he didn't believe this, so looked over the rail gate only to find no tire tracks in the snow on the other side. All right, he reasoned. They have another way in. He took the road around the camp, circling slowly, gazing at the sea of virgin snow through the stand of trees. Finally he stepped out and walked about one hundred yards into the center of the grounds. Nothing.

Furious, he thought of McDonald Lodge up on the lake, climbed back in the Jeep and rattled into gear.

The leap of thought that brought McDonald Lodge to his mind was a good one; the road beyond the lodge was closed for the winter, he had not seen the girls on the road as he went toward Apgar, and they could have only escaped by going one other direction, due west toward the Flathead. A fifty-fifty chance that they were at the lodge, then: okay. He drove far above the speed limit, biting on his lip, unsure, the Jeep clanking around him. Finally he got so cold with the top off that he stopped to put it on. Then onward: he pulled into the parking lot twenty minutes later.

Virtually deserted. The clerk looked surprised to see him and, no, there weren't two young ladies registered together, no young people at all, just a few retired couples, in fact, and no one is allowed to see the register, sorry. He gave Baskin a look of suspicion and suggested that he try the lodge restaurant. Baskin took his advice, but it was a vast empty space, rafters looming overhead, soundless of even the least tinkle of a spoon in the distant kitchen.

Not wanting to go home just yet, he drove back to West Glacier and got drunk in the town's other bar. Boilermakers. Seven of them.

Why, he wondered, did those girls do that to me? What art women that I am mindful of them? Strange and hidden, candid and blatant, our delicate powderpuff gentle whores, our tough angry festered flowers, our brutal instructors in eros. Consider Adam: the nobility of his loneliness. With Eve his melancholy tragedy pratfalls into comedy and doom. Consider that waif of a waitress all unbuttoned; Sarah with her whole life bagging around her ankles with her limp socks; Kate with her mind and dear pussy forever inflamed. Another, please, bartender, and put a twist on it. And consider my meager twenty years: entrapped, free, desperate to be entrapped again, stirrings of freedom pricking my prick when I am. It would be difficult enough adjusting to the old womankind, the stay-at-home Jenny who is servant, bedmate, helpmate, and soft destroyer; now we have the sweet Carlas and Pams, out on search-and-destroy missions, full of vampire kisses and revenge, all cool. The old cold war of the sexes heats up, a balance of power shifts, and I know my fate, I suppose: ELDERLY PRODIGY RAPED BY GIRL PACK. My name will become infamous like Fatty Arbuckle's—only in pathetic reverse, bartender— and the detectives will find my stack of old porno books there among my *Scientific American*'s and they'll interview my old landladies in New York and try to link me with a ring of Basin Street homosexuals and women will point at me, jeering with laughter, wherever I go, saying: There he goes, the first male ever to be gang-banged by us. Timid and lost, I'll go underground, then emerge,

172

later, as a shy secretary or housekeeper. A ruined male maid. I don't understand those two. And where did they go?

The bartender refused him an eighth boilermaker on the flimsy excuse that it was closing time. Baskin eased himself along the whirling mad line of stools toward the front door. Touch of snow in the air.

Driving along the wavy white road. Careful not to slip off into the river. One wouldn't want to sober up suddenly like that, for it's bad for one's constitution. And didn't Pammy ease her little hand inside my coat? And didn't they giggle and say groovy and didn't we partake in a little bawdy talk, a little verbal nudging? They asked me twice, three times, and it wasn't even the old con game, the one where the hooker takes your money and disappears and says to meet her at the wrong address, oh no; all this lies deeper, deeper, too deep for novices and horny dupes, and did you arrange this, too, Sarah? Was this one more shortcut system you devised? Are you there, hovering, my great mamaghost? Or are you nicely reincarnated, riding around inside my fate's—whoops, Kate's—lovely body?

Consider the nature of the fuck. One dreams it in one's lonely room before the fact and it's all music and a dance of air and light; one has one's perfect ejaculation and it goes off harmlessly and beautifully into space, orbiting Venus and the distant stars, and one's partner is mystic and true. Then life gently intrudes. Stop now, Baskin, that position hurts my ass. Idle words slung down from the tower with piercing reality. Words with metaphysical dimensions deeper than if she had said softly, "Oh, darling, you are damned to Hell forever. Sorry." One's life and happy dork go limp, one's feelings fall, one's coition cranks to an introspective halt. Or the act itself, far from the swelling harmony of the dance, falters into an off-key, anti-rhythmic half-step. Consider copulation. For some brutes it may be easy like the dumb swing of the bat in a baseball game at old Comiskey Park, but for you, Baskin, clearly, your every wire and cell—your entire hot little computered self—partakes. Kate's every gesture and gentle heave is a message to the brain and memory. Each bump and grind diddles your microcosm. Watch the road, careful. But consider the metaphysical nature of all that tossing and belly bumping: I have brought you the twenty years of myself, precious Kate, my heartlove. My goal is to drive my mind and sense into that arrogant red tip of me, to explode myself into you, impregnating you every time with a piece of myself whatever reception your arbitrary little egg gives me. There: that sticky mess is me. Regard us, please, with comic tenderness or we'll dry up and be gone.

Consider what we have for such a short time. We get sex just at the right time: sooner and we wouldn't have understood it. Later, perhaps, if we're lucky, we won't need it. Consider, then, its splendor: rare, because it's too soon vanished. Consider the fun of it. You go there, I'll go here, last one home's a ninny.

Or consider, oh, the extraordinary fact that sometimes, occasionally, the dream turns real, the music is there, the dance lighter than crystal air takes you away, and you come, you come together, you hear the gathering thump of the universe between you, the old primordial pumping. Oh, Kate, I'm sorry for today. It's justice that those two tarts fucked me like they did and I'm sorry. Homeward bound, if the snow allows it, and, please, no irony, I don't want to hole up at the Addison place again.

Sometime near two o'clock that morning he stumbled through the snow toward the porch and cracked his

174

scarred shin solidly on the first step. He fell back, offering the great northwest a single wailing curse: "Aahhhhh, sheee-it!" Echoes from the valleys beyond.

In the main room he almost knocked over the short-wave radio and did manage to place the antenna in his left eye. His hip squeaked an end table. One shoe thumped down in the hallway, another in the bathroom where he failed to find his face in the mirror. Toothbrush the evidence away, he told himself sensibly, but he couldn't find that either. He sat momentarily on the toilet and considered the nature of considering things once more. Undressed, he looked down at his beer bulge.

Kate lay still as a stone as he crawled in beside her. He regretted that it had been necessary to leave the hall lightbulb burning, but he could risk no further injury entering the sheets.

Awkwardly, his hand crept over and touched Kate hello.

"You're stinking," she snapped at him out of her half-sleep. "You smell like booze and you smell like women."

"I'll be goddamned if that's so," he said tersely, and he turned, pounded his pillow and passed out.

Toward morning he awoke with the first hint of nausea and hangover and there she was, nestled against his shoulder, her long fingers resting gently on his chest.

⊰ XVII ⊱

Midwinter. Outside, the snow edged up the walls of the lodge toward the bottoms of the windows and at night Baskin and Kate were drawn to the hearth where he stacked up oversized logs. The corners of rooms became suddenly cold with pinpoint shafts of arctic air and outdoors the valley howled and whistled.

It was a time of storytelling. They exposed themselves to each other one incident after another, remembrances stacking up between them until they became each other, so that as Baskin told about how as a child he poked around every lab and office on the Chicago campus Kate listened and seemed to see those places with him. And she revealed herself: not just that self she so frequently offered up in summaries (I'm like this, I'm like that), but the child, the girl, the young woman who had existed in real rooms.

When her father came back from the Battle of the Bulge (a head wound, battle fatigue, already an alcoholic) the family had moved into the prefabricated housing in West Dallas halfway between the slums out on Singleton Boulevard and the rows of pretty, middle-class homes of

Oak Cliff. Spiritually, she admitted, it was slummy—though her family pretended it wasn't different from the homes of her uncles and aunts who lived two miles away over near the golf course. On Saturdays she worked for her aunts cleaning their houses. They didn't regard her as a maid, oh no, just as little Katie scrubbing and dusting, doing sweet favors for the allowance her father wasn't able to pay her, and she played with her cousins, sometimes played too long out there in the creek that wriggled through the golf course so that the aunts had to call her inside, but it wasn't bad at the time, she said, and only later, years later, did she know that the aunts didn't like her or her family. She remembered their refrigerators and how they had such unbelievable items stored away in them: ice cream and bottles of pop and all such things that were bought by her father only on special occasions. "We had an ice box, the aunts had refrigerators," she explained, and Baskin tried to fathom this, remembering the overstocked cupboards and shelves and the bulging Servel of Sarah's famous kitchen. Then came the flowering, Kate told him: the sudden pinch of waist and thrust of breast that made her uncles twitch and fall upon their sentences when they spoke to her. She became, by degrees, first pretty, then lovely, then stunning. That slovenly prefabricated duplex became a temple where young boys came to throw themselves down in awkward admiration and on weekends when she went over to visit her aunts the boys would come following, happy and flowing in the rags of West Dallas, like the tail of a bright and dazzling kite. She learned power and formed the adolescent simplification that it came in two distinct kinds: money and beauty. Soon after this, caught unaware of just how powerful she might be, she met Harry. He was twenty, the son of neighbors two prefabbed houses away, and worked as a cowboy and occasional rodeo rider in Oklahoma; she was fifteen, almost sixteen, and it was a summer in which the hot stars riding high above the Texas sky blurred all her plans for her future, all her carefully dreamt plans and the vague sense of destiny she felt her good looks might provide. In the back seat of his 1949 Ford he whispered, "I've got to have you. You know that now, don't you?" He drawled this into her ear so earnestly, in fact, that she wanted to laugh—he told her that he was just plain damned desperate for her—but she consented with pride. No one had ever seen her pretty body and she was ready, she said, and that was it entirely. In two weeks they were married and off to Durant, Oklahoma. It lasted slightly more than a year until she had finished high school.

Back in Dallas for a year, she dated other drawlers, indifferent to them all, though she allowed herself some sex with two or three of them, then she borrowed from her aunt enough money to attend secretarial school. It was given eagerly, she later knew, because the aunts felt that she would be an idiot secretary forever, but she took her skill to Fort Worth, became the secretary to a college dean, and went through college—mainly in night courses —in three years. She had one boyfriend in college, she reported: Bill the basketball player. Other than with this boy she partook of sex only two other times, both times with the dean on his couch; accordingly, she received two salary increases while employed—not that the raises had absolute correspondence to her willingness, she convinced herself. "I thought of myself by the time I left college as a hardened woman," she confirmed. "And I felt I had taken Texas for everything it could possibly give me. I didn't even want a rich oilman husband. Never saw one I'd have. In fact, I knew exactly what I wanted: someone in communications or the arts. So I went to Chicago and four days after I was there I met Ray McCluskey." And en route to her handsome newspaperman, Baskin learned, there were many detours and setbacks, small brutal lessons and continued flowerings; there at fireside they all seemed to come out naturally. He sat beneath the Russell paintings, in sight of that bound set of Sarah's works, the desk that still held a few pages of his equations, the half-empty bag of cement idling by the door, and took it all in. Strange. In the late evenings when they went off to bed he slept with their mutual histories and he could imagine himself in New York, weary from a day's work and another trip to the movies, meeting this dazzling sixteen-year-old Kate transposed to a secretarial job on Fifth Avenue; or he was his small pudgy self and she was a skinny kid of—how old?—about his age, say, and they strolled around that Dallas golf course near her aunts' houses. In their bed, blanketed and warm, as they came together for those last touchings, he would think, ah, Katie, I marry your history and all the women you ever were. And he'd remember the time she had saved four hundred dollars working in the dean's office and her old man took it from her with the lie he'd pay it back; or the summer she worked for six weeks as a secretary for a construction company in Fort Worth and her supervisor wanted to make her—she was only desperate for money and couldn't even think about men, she explained—and his supervisor wanted to make her and when business was off so that they had to dismiss her, the personnel manager who gave her the news that she was fired also comically expressed his desire, saying, "Look, honey, you're goin' to be off work for a few days. Let me put it simple. I could come over to your place any time you say." And she stood up and said, "Oh brother, what good *news!* You're full of good news aren't you?" She rushed out of the office, fighting back tears, not crying, she said, because hardened women just didn't do that.

Ray McCluskey, then: a man on the make in a greater sense of the word. Handsome, tall, stylish, a former radio announcer turned newspaperman out in the Chicago suburbs. When they met he had just sold an interest in the Arlington Heights paper, had picked up a contract for some racetrack publications, and was dickering for another paper: one of those shopping center specials with a smattering of local news, community boosting and full-page grocery and clothing ads. He taught Kate style, or so she claimed: French cooking, at least, a few avant garde books and paintings, geography (she was curiously lacking there), clothes (she already had good taste, just no bankroll for originals or good items), and cars (the Porsche, yes). All this gave him a self-image, and Kate became part of the image, too: she had, in his opinion, a nice voice, long legs, beauty, everything needed to show and tell about. And she started learning from him immediately and liked that. He knew money, news work, and he had plans—enough that she didn't need to remember any of those she lost by meeting and marrying Harry. You don't want to hear all this, she kept telling Baskin there at the fireside, but she went on until she had it all said anyway. She evolved. She started reading classical history and listening and studying baroque music; she started thinking and taking walks and enjoying nature without Ray's country club tinkling in the background. For a time, her husband enjoyed her evolution. ("Look, honey, I'm fanning out your baroque record albums here on the coffee table, so the Whalens and the Donovans can see what you're interested in.") But then the wedge began. She had surprises for him, he had none for her.

"You surprise me all the time," she said to Baskin, telling him all this. "Your trip to the glacier, for instance. Or the walkway you built. Or the equations on the desk."

And so the end of the story: meeting, marriage, melting away. Years in the process, but there it was: she was trapped by the mind, too, just as Baskin had been, all locked up where Ray couldn't find her anymore. She spent more time at the newspaper office, then, and listened to more of Ray's excuses about why he couldn't get home at night from business conferences down in The Loop. She stood by the wire service reading news releases or slumped in her office chair, book in hand.

"I want this to be a first-class paper," she told Ray.

"No chance, baby. We can't buck the *Tribune* or the *American* or the *Sun-Times* and we're not even going to try."

"So what'll we print? Boy Scout news and the results of the Soap Box Derby?"

"That's it, baby. Sorry. We're not in this like you think."

"Let's start another paper, then, Ray. Something intelligent."

"Something with Walter Lippmann and a bright column of editorials?"

"That's right."

"Forget it. Get realistic."

But she could not get realistic, so that was it. "I want to write and do something just a little important," she told Ray. "So, please, no alimony. Just give me another kind of chance and write me that letter of recommendation. I've *got* to *leave*." Mexico, then. The long Porsches-cape. The baker on the beach. Slow days of feeling the earth turn under her. Do you want to hear all this, Baskin? Yes. Do you want the part about the baker again?

Yes. Do you want every detail? Yes, yes. Baskin, there's some of this I thought I'd never say out loud.

As she talked, the dead of winter closed in. Animals appeared on the porch to escape the blizzards: a pair of young deer banging their feet and clomping around, the wary snowshoe rabbits, a hawk nestling under the eaves of the roof, and, once, an otter—fierce and hungry and lost. Baskin and Kate wore their coats indoors, paced the rooms, checked the thermometers outside the frosted windowpanes, prepared food, fell into minor arguments and reconciliations, but mostly they drifted with a music of nostalgia and memory.

"Why *do* you tell me all this, if you don't want to?"

"Because you've opened a gate in me again."

"How'd I do that?"

"I don't know. But it's great, Baskin, what you've done for me. If I have to face the real bastards of the world again, I'll remember this and you and maybe it won't be so awful again."

"There won't be any others, will there?"

"Well, just *if* there ever is, I mean."

"Say there won't be."

"No, there won't. The gate's open for you, no one else."

"Bite me right here and say it again, please."

"There won't ever be anyone else. Am I biting you correctly?"

"Hey, open up there."

"Hey, yourself. What're you doing?"

"Discussing the future with you. There."

One day there was a break in the weather and when the sun poured out over the surrounding mountains they found they were restless to go someplace. They talked about a trip. In a few days the new year would come, a new decade arriving, and they felt if they could only steal away south—Acapulco or the Bahamas, someplace—to celebrate this event they would be much better for it. But what about Sarah's wishes? Would it be all right to cheat for a couple of weeks?

"We could call Neuborn," Baskin suggested.

"Hell, let's leave him out of it."

"Right. There isn't anything illegal about our leaving."

As they discussed it, a letter from Dierker came.

Isalatoes: Why don't you come to NY for the New Year with me? I'm busy, but I'll be staying in the city for a few days after the 1st with nothing to do. I could buy you dinners, shows & nite life & we could talk body mysticism—remember? —& pantheism & walk the streets, if you want, to get the feel of the pavement & those good deep breaths of soot 'n smoke. I mean it, silly as this sounds. Can you give me a call? JU 6-9797.

I love you both: D.

Oddly enough, Baskin considered that they should go, but Kate didn't want to. In the end they decided on Mexico for two weeks and began calling the travel agent down in Kalispell to make plans. Baskin first decided to call Dierker and offer an excuse, but that didn't seem right either so Kate wrote a short note.

"Funny, I think we should call Neuborn about this," Kate said. "I know what I said before, but now I think we should."

The day before they were scheduled to leave Kalispell, then, Baskin gave Max Neuborn a call.

"No problem at all," Max assured them. "In fact, let's face it: this matter of the two of you staying up there all this hard winter isn't really binding. Personally, I'm a little surprised that you're there." He talked on, making excuses for not seeing them and suggesting that they stop off for dinner when they came back. His tone was professional—only slightly warm—and Baskin wondered why they called. Then at the end of the phone conversation Neuborn said as an afterthought, "Oh, yes, I have your other letter from Sarah. And the original copy of the one that constituted the will, too. You can pick those up when you come back, too."

"Sarah has another letter for me?"

"It was to be given to you at the end of your year up there. But, as I said, there's no reason why we can't play everything loose. She played things that way herself, didn't she?" He attempted a laugh.

"Why didn't you mention the letter before?"

"She told me not to. But now, as I say—"

"We'll wait until the end of the year," Baskin snapped.

"But we don't *need* to! You know how Sarah's dramatic gestures were and how she—"

"We'll wait," Baskin said, and that was it. When he hung up, then, he felt sick at himself for not keeping each one of Sarah's silly wishes and he felt mad at Neuborn, whom he didn't like anyway. He even wondered if he could make the trip, but there was Kate all packed and excited so he didn't say anything.

En route to the west coast of Mexico—in all the airport bars and restaurants and strapped in their seats on the planes—thoughts of Sarah, Dierker, Neuborn, the ranch, everything tugged at him.

At the resort it rained. Great swollen pavilions of clouds rose on the Pacific horizon and drifted in to drown the beaches and patios and golf courses, so that Kate could only finally say, "Well, it's *warm* rain." One day, playing the dreamy lovers who didn't care, they even went out walking in it, but in fact they did care and came back drenched and out of sorts with each other.

They tired themselves making love. Too much of a good thing, Kate observed. Peasant recreation in expensive rooms, Baskin agreed. Then on the fourth day the rain stopped and the verandahs steamed and the beaches pulsed with humidity. They strolled around shops, made a few indifferent purchases.

"Let's go home," Kate said after that.

"We shouldn't have left the ranch," Baskin said.

"I feel the same way," she said.

Returning to Montana, they were shocked by the overpowering winter. Snow had piled up everywhere in ghostly drifts and all the houses and buildings were fat with it, smoke curling from the chimneys. By the time they reached the ranch they were in the doldrums, weary and fussy again. The argument settled on money: why they wasted it on a trip which they didn't want to take (she blamed him for suggesting it) and how the estate would finally be settled (she didn't want him to just write her out a check and pay her off) and how exactly Sarah meant for her part to be paid.

"She just wanted things fair," Baskin contended.

"Oh, she didn't think out details. Because she didn't really *care* about her estate. This year—in her mind, at least—had nothing to do with a financial legacy anyway. It was something for you—"

"What was it for me?"

"Sex education, I suppose. I can't think of anything else to call it."

"I suppose the two of you worked that out?" Baskin yelled at her.

"Well, she wasn't pimping for me, if that's what you mean!"

"I didn't mean that, but you've been damn well paid if that's so!"

185

"You *bastard!* You wouldn't know love if you fell into it!"

"Oh, I know *love!* But I know all this bitchy bullshit when I hear it, too!"

"You know nothing about love—or life. You live between your cold little ears!"

Quickthought: I'm fighting Katie the scrubber, Katie who loved daddy who loved the bottle, Kate who found the cowboy empty and the entrepreneur without mystery, my liberationist, my occult seeker, my free winger who is shackled to herself.

"And where do you imagine *you* live?" he was shouting at her. "In your sensitive nerve ends? In your hot, pulsing little heart where love is true and eternal?"

"I know I'm capable of love! I know I am!" Her scream was somehow suddenly plaintive and pleading.

"Then you know I love you!"

"Yes, I suppose so. In your way."

"All right, but you know it!"

More quietly: "Yes, okay. I know it, Baskin. I'm sorry, of course I know it."

❧ XVIII ❦

He sat by the bay window, equations spread before him, thinking of that lunch with Professor Behrman on the day he learned about Sarah, and he recalled Behrman's sexual condescension, how the old guy nagged him about going down to the French Quarter, and he knew that he had changed so much that Behrman couldn't do it now. I am a slimmer and more worldly Baskin, he assured himself; I hardly stutter anymore and seldom spill my food at the table. And he pictured himself gliding into the laboratories, Kate on his arm. She would be wearing that furred parka she wore that first night at the airport and she would push it back and shake her dark hair loose and smile and the Bunsen burners would ignite in a salute. Or he would visit the old Chicago haunts, nodding hello to those girlish lab assistants, and Lothridge and the others would get nervous and knock over racks of test tubes when they saw Kate and she would take their hands to calm them, smiling at them, but they'd break into stutters and bite their lips. Lovely daydream.

Sitting there, his equations staring up at him, a misplaced and nearly lost emotion stirred in him: he felt curious. He considered the nature of light rays—which related to some of his ruminations months ago about measuring the age of the universe—and he was thinking kinetic energy, diffraction, de Broglie, Rutherford, the Doppler Effect, the Compton Scattering, Dirac, photon clouds, Einstein. Was there a primordial flash, he wondered, which gave birth to the universe? And would the waves and photons of this big bang be stronger as the earth turned toward the explosion in its trip around the heaven, so that if we could determine the excess of radiation caused by the earth's own motion, we could, in fact, measure the motion and therefore the time of this old blast? Superclusters and galaxies, yes, but what of the nature of light? Particles or waves or both? And can they be captured and studied? How to do it?

He stopped. The question of what to do with myself is totally banal and irrelevant; intelligence isn't even intelligence unless it knows what to do with itself. I need to get back to work.

So simple.

Kate came to his side, standing with a bare arm gently around his shoulders. Calculations and flashes of possibilities drifted in his head, though, and he was wondering how to use them, how to get at the photon mathematically. Then: measuring the age of the stars, ah, and that ancient gaseous swirl long before these mountains came into being: what a strange mysticism in that, what wild philosophical musing. Science and the soul, mind and feeling: all things move, at times, into curious unities. He wished he could find the words to say all that he felt to Kate.

"What're you thinking about?" she asked him outright.

He gave her thigh a soft pat, not answering. Curious unities. Sarah reached this same plateau of imagination;

she must have. I blamed her for living in her gut emotions, but she knew calculus, some astronomy, physics, and she was better at geology and botany, by far, wasn't she? She sensed how the universe—from that distant cosmic upheaval to the function of the liver—is all linked up. Didn't she try and talk about this all the time? Body mysticism: didn't she give Kate that legacy to ponder? Sense your body, its rhythms, its capillaries pulsing, its atoms alive, its chemistry boiling and working, and you have a metaphor for existence and can begin to comprehend many things: isn't that exactly what she urged?

Kate stroked his hair, his ears, but he was remembering Sarah's concept of personality—yes, she even had a philosophy of psychology—and how she explained it to him in terms of his clusters. "You file away each piece of information you receive on a person, say," she used to tell him. "Okay. But when you have, say, five facts you actually have more than that—because of the combinations. In fact, you have twenty-five clusters, or five times five, and only there do you begin to sense how dynamic a life is. Man is a complex, each of his parts modifying every other part constantly. That's what being alive is: this swirl of self." She used the word *swirl,* he recalled. Like the gas in a distant galaxy.

"Hey there," Kate said, breaking his reverie again. For the first time he noticed she was naked. She leaned against his arm, so that he felt her hairs, all soft; he patted her again and smiled.

Swirl of space, spiral of time, the dynamism of the world's body. You start, he mused, with the ends of the universe, perhaps, and work down from the major concepts into those small scientific observations where most physicists and chemists and all the assorted technicians spend their lives. If all the world is a gigantic whirling

189

atom, you begin with its greatest part, perhaps, instead of focusing on some tiny interrelationship. Knowledge works two ways: from microcosm to macrocosm, but also from the boundaries of infinity down to the smallest and most infinitesimal part. So I begin way out, perhaps, musing on the big bang theory, how worlds were born in that great primeval flash, but all life is an explosion, too, Sarah, and we're all fragments of it, hurling along in the vast liquid that space is, turning and exploding inside ourselves as we go, burning like the singular embers of the great fiery opus. Ah, Mama: you didn't have a language to express all you knew, hence all your mystic moments and words; but you sensed the harmonies and I do, too. I know more than I know; I'm greater than my clusters. Among them, maybe, as they bounce against each other, the nature of my work will come to me. My life is there, tossing them up in small mental blasts, scattering them, letting them fall, reading their tumbled messages as one might read the runes thrown down.

"Hey again."

"Hey, Katie," he said absently, patting her once more.

"Hey." She wanted him to get up and go into the bedroom with her.

But more: Einstein's famous formula $E = mc^2$. Matter disappears under certain circumstances, yes, and is replaced by energy. So with Sarah: she's gone, but her force field remains. Exploded into nothingness, she still bombards me; my leaps of thought, put into motion by her years ago, still soar on. Her ridiculous mysticisms and my trusted science: the same, aren't they? Just as light is seemingly both waves and particles, undulatory and corpuscular.

"Say there." Bowing her body toward him, she nudged him again.

He kissed her just below the rib cage. "Not just now, Kate," he said, and with that he dismissed her.

The truths of science aren't even truths—all right, the last fifty years of experimentation and quantum mechanics and relativity have told us that. Scientists aren't uncovering hard facts about mass and energy; all that is gone and there's no hard-core physical laws we finally know, not really. So what now? The distant nebula, time itself, the darkest crevice of the brain, the body's wondrous pulse: among such problems what can I be? I can't be a cold and unblinking surveyor of it all anymore, no, Sarah, so maybe I can warm up to the universe and pulse with it and let out my equations like music. *Space is curved,* Einstein told us, and that's a line of poetry; could I become a singer of numbers? Do you understand that, Sarah? Could that do it for us?

He went to the window. The familiar meadow.

Space is curved, time is a bent mirror showing us—to our shock and amazement—that there's no rules or laws. Not mass, not light, not the wandering gasses of space, nothing adheres or holds, and we get thrown down onto it—don't we, Sarah?—with a puny language and grasp. Our myths and metaphors turn out to be wrong, our numbers mesmerize and lie to us. Sarah, an image: running in the meadow, those comic fat tits banging against her stomach as she ran. My rowdy inventor spinning out lowly cowboy stories, creating all she touched, me and Kate and my sad daddy.

Baskin went down to the river. Aimlessly, he walked the rocks at the water's edge. The warm sun fell on him and seemed to heat him to the marrow so that he felt oiled and hot inside, as if all his machinery turned and spun and as if he were at work again.

❧ XIX ❦

The weather offered up a series of warm days, like bright
islands in the midst of the lingering winter, so that Baskin
remembered that same sort of day months before just
after Sarah's funeral in April; a hint of spring rode the air
and between the snow patches an earth of sweet decay
and scented mulch showed itself.

He and Kate went up to an old deserted ranch near the
Canadian border late one morning. She had a cold—a
nagging sniffle which had hung on for days—but wanted
to get outside away from her medicine bottles and salves,
so they got into the Jeep and rode up to this infamous
ruin of the Northfork. A gambler, once, had started to
build a speakeasy resort up there, but nothing had come
of it. An airstrip had been cleared, a great lodge built
with massive logs, a few outbuildings, but it had all been
abandoned. Later, a hermit had taken up residence in the
skeleton of the place. Now there was nothing; those oversized buildings spread out beside the meadow in a stand
of pine like an ancient dream.

They toured the giant rooms, dark rafters menacing
overhead, broken glass and silt around their feet. The

frozen animal droppings revealed that some of the wood's creatures had visited from time to time. A wall calendar announced September, 1931.

"A big idea, all this," Baskin noted.

"There's some gossip," Kate said. "The hermit who came here, according to the story, was the old gambler's son. The son went to prison, then came here after he got out."

Quickthought: myths everywhere, and the question's always the same: what exactly happened, oh, what happened?

Baskin walked around measuring the girth of the massive logs with his outstretched arms. "Like Stonehenge," he marveled. "How'd they get logs this size cut and hauled?"

Kate shrugged.

Exhilarated, Baskin paced off the dimensions of the lodge.

Kate sneezed, dabbed at her nose with a tissue, managed a smile for him. Then she walked outside where she discovered a wide tuft of soft dried grass in the sunlight beside the lodge. When she went to the Jeep to get the blanket, Baskin knew what she wanted, how new places and situations excited her. "Your cold'll get worse," he warned her when she peeled out of her clothes, but she paid him no attention.

Kneeling between her legs, he allowed her to take him in her fingers and use him as she wanted. She rolled his hardness around the edges of her opening, warming the tip of him. The sun beat down through the cool mountain air on his back and he saw her thighs glisten with small glassy beads of perspiration, but he was thinking about this place, how dreams and plans come and go, and he considered one of his idle fancies: the one about starting a retreat for scientists and thinkers up here, but she moved him inside so that he bent and kissed her. Give Katie a little attention now, he reminded himself, as he moved on her. Her face: lips slightly open, dark eyelids closed, all dear. After a moment he turned her on her side, keeping himself thrust up inside her, and moved his fingers into her. Groaning, she nuzzled and kept his rhythm and he looked down on her with a pleasant objectivity, thinking, ah, sex is good for you, Kate, you love this don't you, you love the male and all the tension and sweet battle fatigue of trying to cope with him? It amused him, having this friendly knowledge about her outdoors like this. Odor of pine and the warm brown grass. The distant sound of wind on the slopes, the closer pant of her breath, a word he didn't quite hear. Sensation waylaid him and he smiled, giving her a tender driving fuck, a little body music, but his thoughts went spinning, saying, build that rock walkway out beyond this valley, touch some distant bases with it, construct a dream or two that would make Sarah proud. He watched himself watching: a soft, hot, horizontal dance, Kate following his lead, a long quiver and spasm beginning in her as she bent like a bow. "Oh, Baskin." He smiled at his name being pronounced. "Oh." She was away, floating and gone and he laughed out loud at his achievement.

Standing up, he stretched out his arms with a grin.

"What about you?" she asked, lounging there.

"I was thinking about this place," he said, obviously happy, but preoccupied.

"Come on, now!" She pouted and sprawled there for him.

"Really. I'm wondering why we don't do what I suggested." He told her about his plan again, how he knew so many teachers and researchers who would like a place to get away and ponder some of the tougher mysteries. The photon, electronic impulses in the brain, life on other planets, the nature of the cell, even clairvoyance and extrasensory perception: they could jabber over all those dim mysteries, he explained, and have some drinks and sleep in the mountain air away from their sooty class-rooms and cloisters. She listened, legs raised and opened.

"You've got a super body now," she told him, as he pa-raded above her talking.

But he talked on. "We could build some extra bunk-houses," he said, "and maybe a library. I wonder how much money it would take? I wonder if we could get, say, Lothridge and Parmelee to throw a little into the project?"

"This is already a definite project?" she asked, smiling.

"Sure," he said, and he dropped down and gave her cheek a kiss.

"Come on, now, let me do you," she whispered.

"I'm serious about this," he assured her.

"I know, but come here. Give me it."

"Not now, don't be greedy."

They dressed and went back to the ranch. That night Kate's fever came back and her eyes and nose reddened and puffed; she blamed Baskin for making matters worse. "You let me get cold there on the ground," she said, and when he argued with her she accused him of not caring about her anymore. "If you won't let me help you out, you're just not interested," she said. "It's not like you just have to satisfy *me*. It's not so important that I get mine."

"Oh, who says so?"

"Well, it isn't! You're supposed to be the one who's all hot and bothered for it!"

"I like it. But there's other things, too, damn it! I got to thinking about what to do up here today! You haven't even said how you like my idea."

She sneezed. "Great. Marvelous idea. I'm going to bed and you can dry up before I'll offer you any again."

"You're just feeling bad."

"Don't patronize me!"

"Well, you are. You've got a fever."

"I've got a bad head to think of staying up here with you anymore!"

"Oh, what kind of talk is that?"

"It's true!" she said, and she bit her lip to keep from wailing. "In a little more than a month you'll be gone and I'll be gone and I don't know why we shouldn't call it quits anytime now! You make me sick!"

"Don't cry, for god's sake."

"I won't, don't worry," she said, starting to cry. "It'll be a long damn time before I'll cry over a man again."

In spite of all, he felt complimented. A man, yes. He had the urge to take her wrist and bend her down, to do something masterful and heavy. But he said, "The idea of this retreat—"

"Oh, stuff your big ideas!"

"The idea of this retreat would be—in part—to keep us together. If I go back to work someplace at a school, I mean, I'd always come back here in the summers. And somebody'd have to run things. It would be awfully hard doing it—much more than caretaking. We'd have to have cooks again and ranch hands. Yet it wouldn't last all year, either, so you could have your time to yourself."

"Oh, I'm going to bed," she told him.

"It would be the sort of thing that Sarah—"

"Good night," she said, cutting him off.

He wadded up a piece of paper on his desk and slammed it into the wastebasket. Then he sat quietly.

Listening to the shortwave that night, he recalled the old gang: Sarah's naked troops. It tickled him to think of Mrs. Parmelee jiggling around the ranch with Mrs. Ludmiller while down on the sundeck getting dazzled by Kate their husbands would be trying to keep their thoughts on the mathematical heights. He played himself a game of chess, musing as he moved around the table to parry himself. If Sarah were here, the professors could come out to get laid and rejuvenated; great scientific humpings and pensive affairs in the old stables, on the river banks, in these worn rooms. The required course would be one night at the Addisons', one morning at the old deserted ranch, once in the stables, twice in the bunkhouse and ten or twenty good screws here in the main lodge. The world would surely benefit: a new cosmology, a new humanism, science rededicated, mankind restored at Sarah's and Aphrodite's Summer Festival. Of course, the social scientists would want in. Also the artists. We'd have to buy up all the land on the Northfork and throw up roadblocks.

Less frivolously, then, he thought of Sarah and that old community of friends and strangers, those nights at fireside when they were dressed and formal and conversing in what seemed now to be an old lost dignity. Beyond desire, beyond the overt manipulations. It was real, wasn't it, that company of harmonious people with their music and food and tender naked display? It was true, wasn't it, that with all Sarah's faults and eccentricities she made society possible? A society: lives brought together.

Thinking on this, he looked up to see Kate standing there in the doorway with her nightgown clutched at the throat. "Dierker," she said. "You should certainly tell him about your idea."

"Why? What for?"

"Believe me, what he wants from you is the opportunity to help with something you want. He's asked you for money, now you should ask him."

Baskin went over and gave Kate a hug. Her hair smelled of sun and honey. "How're you feeling?" he managed.

"Lousy."

"Let me fix you a toddy and give you a rub."

"No, that's all right."

"Oh hell, let me pamper you. I need to."

❧ XX ❦

Winter hung on, Kate's sniffles worsened, so Baskin went down to Kalispell alone to talk with Max Neuborn. On the way down he stopped off at the Addisons', thanked them for their absentee hospitality months back, accepted a cup of coffee, and heard old man Addison instruct him in community matters: the meeting hall, mail deliveries (someone had a petition for more service and never mind the roads), and the spirit of neighborly snow dozing. Baskin listened, sipped, and took a jar of Mrs. Addison's apple jelly with him when he left. Then in town that afternoon he told Max Neuborn that he wanted cash for some new construction up on the property and asked about local architects. Neuborn, officious and unblinkingly serious about all these money matters, answered with ceremony, and after a while Baskin was sitting there observing him, trying to imagine once again why he disliked Neuborn so much. A vest: perhaps that. Neuborn was too young for a vest just as he was too shallow for the resonant voice he tried to muster while talking business. Also, ah yes: he didn't approve of Sarah, he had a prissy little wife, a brother-in-law who belonged to Mensa and leered, a distaste for everybody who didn't fit his concocted and conservative notions of what life up in the valley should be.

Baskin stood in the doorway trying to get away while the lawyer discussed the merits of this or that architect. Finally, Neuborn said, "Oh, the other envelope. Let me get it for you." And he was off before Baskin could refuse, so Baskin decided to take it with him—take it and not open it until the appropriate time. It promised little, anyway: a small envelope (the sort invitations are mailed in), thin, just a note or less.

The rest of the afternoon Baskin spent at the office of a young, bedraggled architect just out of school and without commissions: the one Neuborn recommended least. His name was Peter S. Stone and he had an office at the feed store. "You have a name of an architect, anyway," Baskin remarked about his circumstances, and the young man, of course, didn't laugh. But as they talked about the project all sorts of possibilities arose (an underground hallway between the buildings, construction out of lodge poles and native rock) and Baskin liked him very much. The first plans could be ready in two weeks, Stone said. All right, but I want tentative sketches sooner. Agreed. And I want things laid to scale, so come to the property. Too much snow, but, yes, agreed. Tomorrow: yes. They haggled and fussed and bargained, but with warmth, and once Baskin asked, "Do you know who I am?"

"I haven't the least damned notion," Peter S. Stone said.

"And you've never heard of my mother?"

"Your mom? No, why?"

"The writer. The nudist."

"Never."

Aside from this, Baskin won all the negotiations except

one. He wanted to write out a check as a down payment on all this high-sounding activity, but Stone wouldn't take anything. "I don't take money for work yet undone," Stone said, exposing sudden principles.

"You don't have a single commission," Baskin argued. "You admitted it yourself."

"That doesn't matter."

"Also, you'll have expenses driving up to the ranch."

"How much were you thinking of giving me?"

"A thousand dollars."

"Well, I'll say I'm not interested anyway."

Baskin explained that the money would just lie in the bank, but it was no use. Stone clearly needed money (odor of grain and fertilizer wafted over his drawing board), but there matters stood, so Baskin drove back up the Northfork.

Back at the ranch he became so excited that he felt like Sarah among her nitwit projects. About this time of year, he recalled, she planned and hustled, wrote friends in New York, bounced around like a physical education director. Until Peter S. Stone got there a few days later, then, Baskin could hardly contain himself.

Kate, Baskin and Stone went out into the soggy meadow to take photographs. The tunnel here, the new cabins there: much talk. Stone announced that he would do all surveying himself. A scale model, they agreed, had to be built and Baskin proposed to do that himself.

"No, it has to be done right," Stone said.

Miffed at this, Baskin assured Stone that he was capable.

"You have no experience," came the rebuttal.

"Better leave him alone, if he says he can do something," Kate said, coming to Baskin's defense.

They walked and made fevered pronouncements and

dreams. It was another of those days when the weather peeled back to expose an onrushing new season and they sloshed through melted snow puddles, took photos of the river and meadow, every rise and stand of tree, and had supper when finished. By this time Kate was calling their architect Pete. A nudge of jealousy—the same he felt briefly with Dierker—bubbled into Baskin's thoughts, but his enthusiasms dispelled all that. He talked about Stonehenge, bridge building, temples in the sun, spewing out his feelings so that, once, Kate said, "I've never *seen* you like this, never," and the evening passed with Baskin being expansive, making declarations, spinning out optimisms. Stone, caught up in the tempo, chalked the dream on the blackboard: a network of lovely stone and log over and underground with deep warm apartments beneath the snow and buttresses of glass opening up vistas across the meadow and mountains. And they were talking about why: exactly why Baskin wanted such a place for a scientific community which had its academies and offices. Because: you think better alone while surrounded by others. Because: all thought modifies all thought and we need wild theories in collision as well as good solid logic. Baskin explained and explained until they were all smiles, warmed and brandied there at the hearth, and he said, "Also, I'm bringing the world up here to Kate so she won't have to go back after it."

She put her hand on his. "Oh, that's the nicest thing you've ever said," she told him.

Near the end of the evening Stone talked about himself. He had kicked around various schools, stopped his education to become a contractor and builder (". . . architecture is three-dimensional, and you only learn that by putting up real structures.") and finally went back to finish a degree at the University of Montana. "Now I'd like to build things out here in the open so that travelers will come on them suddenly and gasp," he said. "Like seeing ancient ruins in the raw desert or jungle: that's the sort of emotion I want to give everybody." Baskin listened, thinking how infectious all dreams are. Then they were at the door saying good-bye and there were handshakes, promises, mutual encouragements passed around.

Baskin's next days filled with chores: letters to the cities of his life reporting on this newfound dream and enlisting followers, instructions to the dismayed ranch hands who wandered back to find a heavy spring and summer schedule awaiting them, even musings over a new set of equations growing at his desk. Not the least of this newly busy life was Kate, who now, toward April and at the end of their year together, both fretted with vague dread and showed more and more enthusiasm for the building project.

Stone became a frequent visitor, delivering his plans and chatting away whole afternoons, and Baskin, refusing any help, went about constructing the model of the retreat there in the lodge's main room. The ranch hands built a platform—about the size of four card tables—and Baskin duplicated the landscape: bend of the river, rolling meadow, clump of pines. Devising a scale, using the available tools of drawing compass and string, he molded the tiny terrain with plaster and watercolored it green. (My old easel, my frayed childhood brush.) On this he began putting together a model of Stone's drawing using pebbles, toothpicks, scraps of cardboard and wood, and in the intricate work, bending over all this for hours, he enjoyed a happy mindless release and the same sort of pleasure he had felt building that walkway outdoors. Kate stood there and marveled at him.

And, at times, he felt transported and moved beyond

himself, his memory flailing at him as he worked at this toy dream (my medieval soldiers: I cut up tin cans for their armor, remember?) and he could imagine a boy—his distant small self—sitting there on the floor beside him and Sarah standing just over there, wetting the pencil tip on her tongue while she jotted down another cattle rustling or saloon scene. Again, once again: Sarah ebbed back into his head, leaking the old life into his system once more. Her socks, novels, tubby brown body, bribes and cram courses: everything came back in one long meditation of days as he glued and pieced things together from Stone's drawings.

Mainly, the days at Chicago came back to him, and he could ask himself now that small and overwhelming question: what went wrong between us? In that apartment on Kimbark Avenue, in those labs, at those ball games and musical concerts, somewhere, somehow a circuit failed; the peer group entered, yes, and Sarah embarrassed me, he could tell himself, but it wasn't simply that she made herself ridiculous around my professors and buddies. Her love changed: that was it. When her possessive love ended, another sort of love didn't come to fill its place; she doted on her early creation, didn't understand when I became another Baskin, all free and different. And I had my own failure of understanding, too, because at that moment I retired her from her tutorial job and didn't understand how lonely, how silly and useless and wounded that left her. So the parade of men came, days of bungling efforts to ingratiate herself with the profs, even a newspaper ad, finally, begging for help: Wanted: Friend: To Help With Job I Can Already Do Perfectly Well Myself. Desperate Working Conditions. Uncertain Benefits.

Cluster: Kate arrived and looking back now, sure, Sarah must have been amazed to see her—trim and pretty and not too smashed up by her journalistic career—answering that classified ad.

We went for a picnic in Jackson Park, sitting out there one afternoon with all the spades leering at us, these two women, one sleek and lovely with her knees and thighs exposed as she sat there idly on the spread-out blanket. Dusk fell and the birds went winding above us, going to roost, gliding, and I remember being apprehensive, and thinking, oh, what if that gang of bucks shooting basketball over there decided to come over and wise off? What would I do? Dazzle them with my brainwork? Hardly. I'm half a man—fifteen years old, pimply, stutter-prone, cerebral—and I couldn't say anything in defense or do anything and, oh, I've got to stop looking up Kate's dress, I must stop.

Cluster: Sitting on lab stools with Weihmeyer and Burgess when Sarah became the topic of conversation.

"Don't worry, my old lady's a kook, too," Burgess remarked.

Baskin felt a tinge of injury, an impulse to say something redeeming about her, but didn't.

"My mom is Mrs. Supernormal," Weihmeyer said dolefully. "She bakes goddamn pies for the county fairs. Darns my socks before they've got holes in them. Tells me to keep fit at school."

"My mother's whacky and drove my old man insane years ago," Burgess went on. Then: "By the way, what about your daddy, Baskin?"

"Don't have one. I arrived by accidental insemination."

End of topic.

Cluster: the fifteenth awful horny year: in the midst of it, nagging and fighting with each other the whole time, Baskin and Sarah took a trip. By extracting a promise from him months in advance, she got him to give up working during his spring vacation and go to Key West. "This'll do you good, no kidding," she insisted, so off they went, flying down late one evening, renting themselves a car and a fishing boat (their guide was a skinny Cuban with a fierce scar and Sarah, Baskin knew, lusted after him mightily) and doing the scene. Sarah caught a barracuda ("It figures, Mama.") and Baskin sunburned himself over a weekend of bouncing around the Gulf Stream, and during the days they visited Audubon's house where Baskin rather enjoyed lecturing his mother on the artist and the military museum and the shrimp boats at dock. At night, after they had stuffed themselves with conch chowder and lime pie, Sarah urged him to go out alone for a stroll—curious of her, that suggestion—so he obeyed. He went walking around the hot streets, thinking of women as he supposed she wanted him to think, but naturally he was pudgy, baby-faced and as inept as usual and couldn't even gain admittance to the bars where, he surmised, some of the world's saltiest women hung out. Painful, all of it. Stupid. Wishing that he had stayed at the lab, he went down to the Aquarium and watched a fat jewfish loll around. Taking the tour train out to the jetty one evening, he stood looking out over the placid water feeling pure loneliness. In his head, the story he had overheard since coming to Key West about how ships used to wreck on the reef out there: after a lighthouse was constructed to keep ships away, the local salvage-minded citizens kept putting out the light so that a few ships would wreck anyway. Good business, that shipwrecking, and, oh, standing there, he made up strained metaphors to fit his melancholy: I am shipwrecked, too, and each time I start to recover myself someone—most often, Sarah—helps to wreck me again. Is this what I have to go through, all wrecked inside so that I can produce and suffer the solitary pulse of genius? O night! O sea and stars! He imagined himself on the beach below the jetty there, shuffling along in the sand, encountering a girl dressed in a sheer white negligee, weeping. Definitely weeping. Or he would be uptown in a cabaret, mad Latin girls in red surrounding him, urging him boldly to have some absinthe and ass, and he would lean on the bar and explain black-body radiation to them and they would gasp and sigh with adoration and amazement. Four times he went out at night like that in Key West and four times Sarah managed to ignore the fact at breakfast the next morning, never asking once what he did. On the fifth day he asked if they couldn't leave—this exotica is killing me, he wanted to say—and visit the space center, so they drove up to Titusville. Good Sarah, he could think now, wanted so much for me, but for years there no matter what she wanted and no matter what I wanted my dork was safely in my own fist at night. I needed to be thrown bodily into some teeming brothel, given over to some kindhearted prostitute, a stern father saying, "Take care of him, Fannie Mae, and treat him right 'cause this is his first," for something had come unplugged in me, some hot wire left unattached, and I wasn't able to do it on my own.

Images, now, of a time all gone: the waterwheel at the river, her old Royal typewriter, a moment on Grinnell Glacier, the wolverine we sighted in the woods. I am wrapped in odors of sulphur and citronella, the taste of veal chops Milanaise and moose meat. And the truth arrives, slightly late and breathless, to tell me its secret: she was tuned into you, always, your Sarah, and in spite of the fact that Key West went wrong, that those long Chicago winters together went wrong, that your adolescence botched itself, she has prepared this for you here, this interlude with Kate, this journey out. Kate suspected as much herself; she knew that Sarah had done this, planning it out since she had time, the cancer gnawing her and her wit working on me the same as ever. How far back, I wonder, did her plan begin? When she first saw Kate, probably, she said to herself: here, this is it: I will throw my baby Baskin in with this wounded female creature who has so much of the hot musk of sex about her. Her warmth will melt his icy little bones, his innocence, perhaps, might even return her to the world of men—if she can glimpse them as the scared and mean little boys they are once again.

So I was set up.

Cluster: just after graduation, after the ceremonies and after our loud argument in the restaurant when I told her that I was going to New York without her, she seemed to settle down. In the few days left she put my clothes in order, helped me pack, boxed up my books. All this helpfulness, perhaps, because she intended to follow me across the continent like a friendly detective. She talked about returning to Montana, running a few horses again, possibly inviting Kate out for a long visit, and our conversations went unusually mild until we were at the airport saying good-bye. There, faced with departure, she had a list of complaints and desires: I should have my laundry done without starch, the shirts hung on hangers just as she always found a laundry to do for me; I shouldn't keep snacks for the afternoon and late at night because my weight would go up; I should see the Mets (they were a nice comedy, not really baseball, she explained to me) and go to Shea Stadium, especially, when our Cubs visited; write letters; don't get sassy with my new bosses and always remember to listen because you don't learn anything when you're showing off your own skills.

"Oh, Mama, Christ, I know all this!"

"That's what I mean: this very attitude is what I'm attacking. You're not Mr. Big out there with these all-pro scientists, believe me, and they don't care if you worked long division when you were four years old."

"My vanity's all that oppressive?"

"Oh, no, sugar, you're all right, but just remember yourself, please, because sometimes you get a little uppity."

"Mama, I'm scared. Believe that. I'll be very respectful."

"Another thing: mess up your life a little, if you can."

"What's that mean? Jesus!"

"Make mistakes, get involved with people. Don't just hang around the labs getting your numbers lined up. New York is a nice big town with lots of ways to screw up and you should find yourself some muddles. Like I did."

"That's a fine thing to tell me."

"A few pratfalls help us. They jar our systems loose. See: you're the worst mistake I ever made and the best thing I ever did all in one."

"Mama, my plane's been called."

"I know, but listen: I've never been on the subject with you exactly—not in a personal way—but, well, take my advice, for instance, and don't wear, that is, don't use any preventive device with any New York girl that you think is nice and—"

"What now?"

"I know this sounds odd, Baskin, and usually mothers would be saying something different under these circumstances, but with you, well, all I have to say is get good and involved."

"Let me get this straight. I'm to knock somebody up?"

"Sort of, yes."

"Sort of knock somebody up, then?"

"Don't put me on. Listen to what I'm telling you—the *essence* of what I'm saying."

"Literally, you're telling me to ruin my life."

Nervous laughter from us both. We were moving down the long concourse toward my plane now, hurrying so that Sarah's socks began to sag, as always, and she was somehow deeply sad in spite of this silly conversation.

"Ruin it, then, okay. You ruin it one way or another, believe me, and you might as well ruin it for a false idea of romance as for a false idea of something else—like your job. I mean, Baskin, there are lots of ways to go crazy. You can adapt yourself to the lab—I've seen this in you—and that's insanity. A form of insanity others like you to accept, as a matter of fact. Choose your poison, I mean."

We stopped as the ticket agent stamped and folded my one-way dream. In truth, I didn't understand what Sarah was talking about, but she kept on; I gave her my cool distant smiling self.

"You write me," she demanded as I stepped inside the waiting area. There was suddenly a rail between us.

"Oh," I said, remembering something. "My old microscope is in the lab at school. My office is all cleaned out, but I left that. You can mail it to me—or tell Lothridge to give it away. I don't care."

"I might take it back to the ranch."

"What for?"

"Well, I might need it."

"It doesn't matter to me. Look, good-bye, the crowd's moving and I want to get a seat by the window."

"Good-bye, then." The crowd nudged me forward, separating us, and she called something I didn't hear. "I *will* take care of the microscope," I heard her say. We waved, our last words concerning an old mechanism, a relic of childhood, and I went through the door without a kiss, without an I Love You, Baskin, and without a Thank You, Sarah. The world closed in. To my relief, I found my window seat so that I could observe the clouds above Indiana and Ohio.

In the room, now, that same microscope sat on a high shelf where Kate had dusted and put it, and there stood the typewriter and outside someplace a remnant of the old waterwheel was becoming dry rot in the heat of a new season. Baskin paused above his model ranch, these and other clusters in and around him, thinking of dinners spent with Sarah after that parting, holidays, briefly, here and there, but mostly that was it: a fading away at a crowded concourse, a sigh of relief at getting away at last.

He got up and went to the calendar hanging on the kitchen wall. March 22. Sarah died on April 4. A year, almost, and it was going to settle into spring and summer more quickly this season. Impulsively, he walked into the bedroom and retrieved the envelope Neuborn had given him. Kate was down at the bunkhouse checking for winter damage, Stone was due to arrive, but for the moment he stood there alone; zipping off the end of the envelope, he shook out Sarah's last message: a card, one of those cards from the Tarot deck. This one—oh, who can stand so much appropriateness?—was The Lovers. Baskin stood there in the dim bedroom light inspecting it. There were two naked figures, male and female; behind each was a tree—the tree of knowledge behind the man and the tree of good and evil behind the woman; beyond the trees stood a sexless angel, wings outspread, and the whole card was bordered with a happy orange. He turned it over hopefully, but it bore no inscription.

Out in the main room he stopped to view his model. Peter would be surprised. Perfect. A job well done, almost finished. He tapped the Tarot card on the east meadow and left it there.

❧ XXI ❧

Details, butt ends, odd jobs: the days filled up.

Letters arrived, from Parmelee (he would throw in some money, yes, and continue Baskin's appointment by proxy), Lothridge (grants and fellowships, sure, he would get those by the fistful, just leave it to him), and Baskin's old employers in New York. Dierker wrote that his firm would do a book on the project, if Baskin would lend his name—remember me, the prodigy?—as author. Come to New York, too, Dierker urged him, and let's talk this out. We'll have dinner at *Le Périgueux.* Perhaps publish an annual of writings from scientists in attendance. Money and business talk. But come, please, this month or next. The ranch, meanwhile, became a hive of people: Peter sloshing around in the meadows with the surveyors, the contractors out there with their heavy boots sucking and sticking in the mire of melted snow, the ranch hands going about their chores with a few sidelong glances at all this activity.

Kate stayed busy, too, though her eyes sometimes asked, *okay, but what about us? It's April and what about us?* She brought her typewriter up from the bunkhouse and became the ranch's corresponding secretary. Down to Kalispell she went—the station wagon threw a rod, so that a ranch hand had to retrieve her in the Jeep—after the letterhead stationery Baskin designed. (There it was, surprise, surprise: THE NORTHFORK SEMINAR, Kate McCluskey, Managing Director, and a list of eminent scientists and friends who had agreed to ride on the letterhead with her and Baskin.) Up the hill she went with the ranch hands and laborers, too, in search of suitable rock. They passed Sarah's gravesite all dotted with early wildflowers. In the evenings, wearied, she helped in the kitchen although she wasn't really needed since the return of the ranch cook and listened to Baskin struggle with the Northfork telephone system as he tried to call new sponsors around the country. The shortwave blared. There seemed to be people everywhere. Peter came and stayed and wouldn't leave until after dark and the ranch hands, as always, asked stupid questions and kept under foot. *What about us, now?* her eyes asked across the room, and Baskin watched and reached out and touched her hand when he could and at night, after his desk was cleared away, he would go in and look down at her sleeping in her exhaustion. One night he shook her softly awake and she murmured, "Hey, I thought you'd given this up," but opened and took him in, and in the morning her face puzzled after him and she was trying to make him out, he knew.

Let her wonder, he had decided. Not that he was malicious or cold, no; his eyes followed her body as it decorated the rooms—lovely pinch of waist, indelicate jut of breasts loose and warm under her riding shirt—and, as ever, he wanted her, but less now and in somehow strange and different ways. Her voice: he needed that. She could idle in the kitchen talking to the help, just so he could listen. Her silent trances there on the rug, too: let her just sit there cross-legged, eyes shut, arms limp, crumpled bare pages around her. (She still couldn't get anything written except, now, his correspondence.) Or her fussiness, even that. At times, as they bordered on an argument, he found that he took an almost unbearable pleasure in it.

"I'm not going to New York with you if you go," she would say, both asking him if he *were* going away and putting up a tough front.

"Right, you stay here and tend to things. Fine." It amused him to avoid her disgruntled probe.

Another time he found her with a stack of scientific catalogs, order blanks spread out, busily at work. "What are you doing there?" he asked, peering over her shoulder.

"Ordering lab equipment."

"How can you do that if you don't know what we'll need?"

"I'm ordering lots of everything. On approval only. We can send back the items we don't use."

"I was going to order the lab furnishings myself."

"Go have an abstract thought instead. Leave me alone."

He left the room with a smile she didn't see.

Soon she had grown completely possessive toward the project and as she signed letters, planned schedules and kept accounts she asked Baskin to please not interfere.

All right, he told himself: perfect.

They continued their joint bank account without any discussion. More than just Kate/Baskin they were a corporate dream, hard at work, each of them so busy that they had no time to mull over their separate natures or mutual destiny. A calm came over them, infected them, so that her eyes no longer seemed to ask *what about us?*

as it became apparent that they were tangled hopelessly together.

One night she kissed his eyes, shoulder blades, the scar on his leg.

One day they argued again. "You've got to stop inviting guests for this summer," she said. "I've got to make plans for food and linens! And the lodge is full because no matter how well the construction goes we have too many guests!"

"I want that astronomer from Australia. And the young German who teaches at NYU."

"Nothing doing! It's a full house!"

"Rent some cots! Put them in the main room!"

"God, you're impossible!"

In the end, she won. He found that he allowed her to modify all his plans to suit herself, but, curiously, she didn't dominate him; instead, her last defenses fell apart now and he saw her at a great, loving, objective distance: she was in the world, back with men and in tender combat again, and caught up in something suddenly useful and important. In spite of such minor and occasional frictions, the calm settled in.

One night, dreaming, he had an elaborate clairvoyant vision of all he would accomplish and be. He would create an equation for the photon and the nature of light which would win him a scientific prize. At an occasion in Geneva in April, 1979, he would address a gathering of philosophers and tell them that philosophy was impossible because language would always be an imprecise form of communication (many illustrations) and the philosophers would tell him to mind his own business. Before this he would marry Kate McCluskey and they would have three children, all normal except for the one who would later write novels illustrated with photographs.

The Northfork Seminar would be written up in *Time, The American Scholar, Scientific American, Punch* and *Nudism Today*. While his family stayed in the New York apartment or at the Montana ranch, he would lecture and do research at Oxford and the University of Cairo, yet he would remain chaste and faithful during such absences. Three of Sarah's books would turn into rowdy westerns produced by a movie mogul in Osaka, Japan. Kate would take up watercoloring and win prizes and acclaim. American politics during the 1970's would return his stutter for a brief visit. He would establish a means of measuring the probable age of the universe—for which he would win an even more famous scientific prize. Tennis and snooker would become his games. A series of sonatas which he composed would go unpublished and without performance. After his fortieth birthday he would fly his own plane, grow paunchy again, and develop an affection for the city of London. A short memoir on Sarah would be published in a thin, overpriced edition by Dierker's firm. Some of the philosophers who reviled him earlier would later acclaim him the new Wittgenstein. He would grow slightly bald, but would wear his hair in a cunning comb job all razored and fluffed. Cambridge would confer a degree. He would prefer sex once a week and about once each month he would get snozzled on boilermakers. The President of the United States would once write him a fan letter. He would become widely known as a conservationist. Astronomy, physics, chemistry, math, logic: he would work at these like an addict to crossword puzzles, filling in the blanks, knowing that all the words said very little. All this, he knew when he was awake, would actually come to pass.

≫ XXII ≪

"Stay away from Peter Stone while I'm gone."

"Why'd you think you had to say that?"

"I don't know, I just said it."

"Well, you didn't have to. I hope you know it."

"To tell the truth, I thought I should—so I did."

"If I'd ever been interested in Peter Stone something would've happened before now!"

"You mean you've been giving each other the sign?"

"No, I didn't mean that!"

"He looks at you like you're a candy bar."

"It's just that I don't wear any underwear and that makes him nervous, but I'm not changing just for his sake."

They were at the airport (yes, again: he felt he recognized the two women in his life at the moment he passed through a turnstile, glimpsing them just as the jets fired him off into space) and having this conversation in not exactly muted tones. Baskin was en route to see Dierker. Kate wore a dress—unusual in itself, but a stylish, short blue sheath which displayed her legs to advantage—and she looked dazzling. In fact, as their voices went up Baskin received a sudden comic picture of them standing there and could imagine some stranger (a practitioner of karate, probably) coming over and clubbing this plump bookworm who was screaming at this magnificent brown-skinned darling. A smile almost took his mouth.

"While we're on the subject," she went on, "stay away from your daddy's playmates!"

"Oh, come on! Not the old counterattack!"

"Why not? You probably brought this up just so you could get your conscience free to do what you want in New York! Don't think I don't know that town! Or Dierker! Or those mopsy little twists who fumble the typewriters in his outer office!"

"You know why I'm going: business. If he does a book on the conference, that's great publicity and revenue."

"That bitch who stripped at Sarah's funeral! I'll bet she's up there waiting to take your dictation!"

"Oh, get off it!"

"You started it!"

They stood under a sign that read AIR WEST and looked through a dirty window out to the runway where the plane—a six-passenger job with numbers all over it—warmed up to take Baskin to his connection over at Great Falls. Not many people moved around the little airport, but those who did gave them cautious glances. As Kate talked, he thought of farewells: Sarah, Parmelee, Kate. All those before had been more final than this (he planned to be back in a week or less), but this one hurt.

"We're messing around in each other's lives too much anyway, I suppose," Kate was saying.

"Huh, what?"

"I said that we're messing around in each other's lives too much. You should go do whatever you want and so should I. After all, we're not married or anything, so I don't know why we're standing here yelling at each other."

"Sarah told me once to go ahead and mess up my life. One way or another, she said, we do it anyway."

"You'll go to New York, I realize, and those girls will be there and either you will or you won't according to circumstances."

"Well, I won't. You're one of my circumstances."

"Big difference that'll make two thousand miles away!"

The pilot ambled by and said, "We're ready when you are, sir," and went through the door toward the plane. They stood there for a moment doing nothing at all, then Baskin took her hand.

"Marriage couldn't make things worse," Kate sighed.

"What does that mean?"

"I'm miserable enough," she explained. "If you *were* my husband it couldn't be worse. I've never been jealous of anyone before and it makes me sick. And I fret about our future. And sometimes I think you don't like sex anymore—you don't need it on the hour like you used to, I mean. And the seminar: it excites me, sure, but if you leave all the work for me to do—well, you just better not."

"I'll give you a call from the East," he said, kissing her cheek.

"Please do," she pouted. "Think of all those mad scientists calling and writing. I'll need your advice."

"I'll be in touch. Promise."

"The Australian wants to bring his wife and four sons. They all like to fish, he wrote me. He was very eager. How do I explain we aren't even *built* yet?"

"We need that Australian, so work it out. Put them on the floor of the main lodge."

"Everybody's on the floor of the lodge already!"

They went through the doorway, arms entwined but snapping at each other. "Everything will work out beautifully," he said, lying to her cheerfully.

On the plane, then, bumping along, he stared down until the mountains ended and the flat wheat fields began. It occurred to him that he and Kate had somehow pledged their fussy affection to each other permanently. There was too much glue between them: Sarah, the ranch, the same bank account, all the private moments stacking up. He rested his head on the seat, closed his eyes. Downward to darkness. A glacier, shy Tina—was that her name?—an old microscope, Sarah's gilded volumes: all this in the black space behind his dreaming lids.

He changed planes at Great Falls, taking Northwest Airlines over to O'Hare in Chicago where he waited around for the final leg of his trip to New York. It was a hot day in Chicago, up in the eighties, and it made him restless enough to walk around aimlessly. He had an ice cream cone and looked at people. Finally, he was strolling around the kiosks and he saw a strangely familiar face. Perhaps. He studied it for some minutes. A young man slumped behind his newspaper, clothes rumpled, scowling.

"Is that you, Burgess?" he asked, going up and sitting in the next chair.

Burgess looked at him blankly.

They had that moment while they pointed their fingers at each other at close range, trying to remember.

"I can't believe it's little Baskin," Burgess said at last.

"It's me all right. How've you been?"

"Oh, well, okay. Yeah, I've been okay." Burgess seemed strikingly different, but kept exclaiming how different Baskin was—which, of course, had to be true. But Burgess had not so much *age* as something else: the set of his mouth, perhaps. They talked about Weihmeyer, how he had a job with an electronics firm in Wisconsin. "You know," Burgess said, "he's the normal type. He has a house, wife, kids, this money we all need. He's grooved himself and that's all right, isn't it?" Baskin agreed that, yes, that was certainly all right. They found themselves with enough time between planes to have a sandwich and a drink, and Burgess found out about the seminar, about Kate, Sarah's death, and started on his own story. He had never finished his degree and had become an academic lingerer occupying the same labs and walkways and coffee houses; he was traveling down to a small, up-tight college in the Midwest, he said, where they didn't care if he had his degree or not, but he lacked enthusiasm for the interview with them and supposed he'd return to the university for another year of poverty as a graduate student, pretty lab assistants, and the climate of political discontent and free love. "You really changed, boy," he kept saying. "I didn't think you'd look like you do."

"How do I look?" Baskin asked him.

"Oh, you know: very sure of yourself, but human. You were a machine when you were a kid. A little fart."

They had a second drink and Burgess went on about himself. He described himself as a total failure, Weihmeyer as a normal human being, and Baskin as a success. "No irony here, believe me," he insisted. "That's the way it is." He described the fine line between the three of them, the infinitesimal difference, the all-important variable, and Baskin became embarrassed listening to him. But then they talked about Ludmiller and some of the others and got to laughing and Baskin recognized the old Burgess, bawdy and true, and his genuine pleasure in seeing him showed through, he hoped, as they sat and talked until Burgess' plane was called. Walking down toward the concourse where Burgess would catch his flight they passed one of those airport haberdashers and Baskin, noticing his old friend's frayed collar, thought of buying him a nice new shirt for his interview: one of those brightly striped yellow button-downs. But they passed on. That would be tampering with what had to be, he supposed. So instead he invited him out to the seminar, but that was no good either as Burgess said, "Aw, hell, let me explain it to you again: I'm a loser. You don't want me out there. I lie in bed at night and think about myself and fathom all the ways I've gone wrong and ask myself why I haven't thrown myself into some decent work—having failed at becoming one of the supreme beings of the world. But it's energy: my energy fails me. I can't jack up the old will and determination. And, besides, life at the lower frequencies isn't so bad: a little coed tail, a few beers, cronies, the great liquid bath of university ideas to float around in. But thanks anyway. You know, I mean it: thanks a lot."

They shook hands and Baskin watched the frayed collar disappear through the gate.

For the next hours, going east, he became terribly pensive and solemn and wanted to see Dierker very much; he could imagine his father's sunny face and could nearly smell those soft tobacco and vermouth odors in Dierker's clothes. Money and business talk, Dierker had invited him to. Yet there would be more, much more: some honesty, if they were lucky.

Drifting up there at thirty thousand feet again, he could count the extraordinary number of people who had suddenly crowded themselves back into his life during that short year of seclusion: Dierker, Kate, Lothridge and Parmelee again, Peter Stone, Neuborn, the ranch hands, even Burgess. And Sarah, of course: she was back in some mystical way. He flew east thinking on this phenomenon and because he had all these people who seemed to care about him, perhaps because he had a little money and mobility, because he definitely had a work to do, because of Kate, and perhaps, finally, because he was a genius, he was in love the rest of his life.